Stephen Airey

Messer Rondo

& other stories by gay men

GAY
MEN'S
PRESS

First published 1983 by Gay Men's Press,
P O Box 247, London N15 6RW, England.

World copyright on the collection © Gay Men's Press 1983:
on each individual work © the author 1983, except
Uncle William and Uncle Robert Take Michael Swimming
© Brilliance Books 1983.

Stories editor Richard Dipple

British Library Cataloguing in Publication Data

Messer Rondo and other stories.
    1. Short stories, English
    I. Airey, Stephen
    823'. 01'08[FS]   PRI309.S5

    ISBN 0-907040-21-7

Photoset by Photosetting & Secretarial Services Ltd,
Yeovil, Somerset
Printed by Book Plan (Billing & Sons Ltd), Worcester

PETER ROBINS
Trilogy: *I. Second Impressions*

Having ordered our lagers, Freddie turned and asked in the same breath my assessment of the political alignments beginning to emerge at home.

"Freddie," I began, then paused to undo one more shirt button and wipe the base of my neck with a handkerchief. He may have attributed my short silence to jet lag or perhaps a wish to formulate some ironic observation. I doubt whether he guessed it to be the exact moment when I understood his chirpy manner and eager questions were a glossy wrapping hiding some deep unease. His private tussles were his concern, yet I found the tensions they provoked in him somehow intrusive. I dismissed my momentary annoyance as a side effect of the dawn flight and a switch of time zone.

"Freddie, you're the political specialist, mate. Shall we take a break? We've had a nonstop giggle all the way from the Terminal at the expense of the bumbling Right and the more idiotic resolutions of the Left. How about filling in on what you've been at these past ten years?"

Two or three hours earlier I would have accepted that he frowned while shaping a crisp summary. That was how he had reacted when I'd asked about hustlers in a square where pop groups stood around slicing the last of the August heat with their music. Now I was certain he frowned because my question, focusing on the personal, had augmented his unease. He said nothing until the lagers had been slapped between us.

"Sure you're really interested?"

The question was witless and I told him so. Seemed reasonable to be interested in what had been happening to someone met at a party ten years back and swiftly steered to bed. Freddie had been fresh-faced then as peaches on a corner stall and worth more than the attentions of some amateur actor who'd been cosseting him in the corner of a chilly lounge.

"We hardly knew one another well, after all."

The evasion and the massive gulp of lager did him no good.

"One full weekend," I countered, dismissing subsequent meals and visits when John appeared predictably half a pace behind. I lit a cigarette and damned the ever more tangible tension in Freddie. My receptiveness to it had to be part exhaustion and part excitement as I absorbed every colour, noise, nuance of this city that lived on a high twenty-four hours a day.

"You're quite right," Freddie was saying with a vehement nodding of his head, "and I don't imagine you remember much of that. I did think you very well-seasoned, I mean, that is, the way you headed us smoothly to the street door and called a cab. No doubt you've been around a bit since then ... you did mention Gerry."

True, I thought, and tried to run a high speed roll-call of lovers through my head, less to flatter myself than to avoid accepting it was not the lager alone that was quenching my thirst. In Freddie's company – hours to be counted on less than two full hands – sharing jokes with him, absorbing a new landscape through a fellow countryman's eyes, hearing him state ideas I myself had so long held and needed to air – I was aware of a deeper relief, of welcome rain on a long-parched landscape. The notion would not be dismissed, however much I concentrated on Gerry back home waiting for postcards. Each minute I shared with gauche, uneasy Freddie it recurred more insistently. Quite suddenly Gerry, like his dozen predecessors, was devalued, became compromises and second-bests for whom I'd settled, conceding that no one could ever measure up to my first love so many decades back. Freddie in one casual meeting had unwittingly disturbed my pattern as I had his.

"I've not been pining in a monastery Freddie – for anyone. You know, I do remember word for word one thing you said" – two but I didn't think it fair to tease him – "We were lying on the duvet that Sunday morning and you said: 'I've never been with an older man before.' Right?"

Freddie grinned, his teeth showing white between two dimples as they had done that evening I'd cut in on the actor dancing with him. And he blushed, just as he had done then, very lightly. His right hand, motionless through the afternoon, other

than to underscore a political inanity as we'd walked through Fifth
Avenue, began to investigate the heavy night air between us with
an aimless television gesture.

"When one is twenty-five in the trendy seventies one
doesn't eagerly admit to being a virgin ..."

"Does one bloody not? You wretch – perfidious wretch.
What about John? What does one have to say about him?"

John, not the forgettable actor but the friend and confidant
I'd never considered to have one flicker of the fire that could
fascinate Freddie. John to whom I'd gracefully given way,
accepting that if he was Freddie's choice then I wasn't into
slouching around for crumbs and if Freddie was happy with his
suburban compromise, so be it.

"You didn't think John and I were lovers? He was a close
friend. Well, he still is."

Again his hand was circling but now the index finger darted
with a tentative, moth-like lunge towards my bare forearm.

"Freddie, you're a monster in blue jeans. Admit you wanted
me to suppose he was your lover. You shared an apartment,
didn't you?"

"Simple economics. We shared political views, nothing else
I assure you."

Maybe it was with the third lunge (I was outraged at my own
past gullibility so didn't count) that Freddie's finger touched my
arm, remaining just long enough to leave a pale impression in my
tan. Pulling back his hand as though stung, he took a further gulp
of beer before speaking again.

"I suppose John was a defence. I mean, I didn't feel I was
experienced enough to cope with any kind of involvement.
Certainly not with you. Hold on – I must have a pee."

As he strode among the tables towards the bar I noticed the
slight thickening of his chest and the way that moonlight, filtered
through dry chestnut leaves, picked out whorls of silver hair that
rested on his almost faun-like ears.

I circled my glass in a small pool of spilled lager and laughed
at the recollection of us both as we had been. Freddie, self-
deprecating about his own body; I myself (as all too often)
overbidding with presents and hospitality until he'd run scared.
So why the hell all this agonising ten years on? If we chose to end a
humid day not with a further pilgrimage among the bright spots
but in Freddie's bed, who'd be harmed? It would be a more honest
celebration than an ever-fulsome good-to-have-caught-up-with-
you-again. Gerry would understand. Even welcome a casual

infidelity to salve his own guilt. What more would it be? At fifty
plus I could do without the pangs of a transatlantic relationship.
And Freddie? He'd hardly bother to mention the incident to one
or other of the married women with whom he lunched from time
to time.

I'd guess I must have been smiling openly into the dregs of
my drink, for when I looked up Freddie was standing among the
shadows from candles on the furthest tables, looking at me. He
seemed not to notice my double-take. In that instant I saw him not
as a lad at an almost forgotten party, but as he would be ten years
on in his mid-forties: jaw darker and shadows round those
larkspur eyes much deeper. I knew then that I wanted him and
would do in twenty years. Whether I sensed or hoped he might
need me, I couldn't have said. He strolled back and sat without
speaking. The whole landscape that began to unfold excited but
scared me and, aware of the immediate chasms, I took refuge in a
joke.

"Freddie, in the past hour you've been for a piss three times.
Bladder trouble in the mid-thirties, or do I still scare you witless?"

"Not at all" – too quick; too slick that response – "It's the
lager. Always has that effect."

And I, conscious of hurtling into the first abyss, didn't press
the question; just as many a romantic, fearing to hurt his lover,
loses his erection when about to penetrate. Freddie pressed his
advantage.

"So where were we then?"

"None the wiser as to who or what you've been up to this
past decade but, meantime, finishing my drink."

Freddie's right hand was now stroking my wrist.

"Like another?"

"Why not? In a gay bar, perhaps."

"Well of course one knows where they are. I mean the area.
I don't mind coming in with you."

The right hand had returned hastily to clutch the lager glass.

"Cut the patronising, Mr Faun Face. One will take one's
bloody visitor in and one will do the ordering. Let's walk."

So we did, among the fancy restaurants, the bistros with
their theatrical facades and the more private faces of houses
where white hibiscus and syringa spattered the stucco with thick
orgasms of blossom. How much Freddie saw I can't say, for he
parried the silence of the side streets with a catalogue of facts
about the architecture and local conservation plans until I
chipped in:

"Why aren't we making for your apartment?"

"Well, as I told you, there are so many books I don't have much room for entertaining."

Our shadows were projected across a terrace of period houses built for founding fathers and early merchants. Until my question we had made level progress. Freddie, agitated by its implications, began to lope ahead, perceiving that his apartment, his tiny English enclave bastioned with rare editions, was under threat. I gave up the shadow play, reached forward and spun him back to me by the elbow. His puzzled glance no longer deceived me.

"If we did go to your apartment we should make love. If we made love we should eventually need a towel but, long before that – probably while you were peeing yet again in the bathroom – I'd have tossed every towel and tissue through the nearest window. Then, at the appropriate moment, I'd rip the innards from the most precious book in your collection and gently, very lovingly, dab you dry with feathery leaves of India paper. How, dear Freddie, would you react to that?"

"I imagine I'd try not to hate you. But I mean, why? Or am I being over-serious again?"

"I was never more serious myself. I'd do it to convince you that people must be the final choice, not books or policies. Not that I could claim people are as handsome or as perfect. Take me – the result of a filthy weekend shared by Edith Sitwell and Bertrand Russell, wouldn't you say? Or take you, standing there like the perennial cricket captain astounded that his rebellious cock simply won't obey the rule books ..."

Freddie, looking somewhere over my head, shifted his weight unhappily from one leg to the other and swallowed. I stretched up the three inches between us and kissed him. Not long or too deeply, but as lightly as his hand had rested on my arm. We ambled slowly away along the rest of the street without speaking, our arms easy round each other's waists. When the last chestnut tree was imminent and we had to emerge under the harvest moon into Christopher Street, Freddie pulled me to him and kissed me until we both knew that to go on we'd need a more private place.

"Still want that drink?" he whispered.

"Not now. Freddie, it would be best if I made for my hotel. I think I should."

"But I thought ..."

"I know what you thought. I don't want a cuddle and an

exhausted fumble. It has to be more or less than that. Anyway, didn't you say before we were out of the airport you were more into girls than boys these days?"

"But you're different – an old friend. I'd do anything ..."

"Bugger the favours, Freddie ... and the boys and girls routine. It's men and women time for you. You're thirty-five this year."

That, I thought, gets rid of a few aces. Still there was no bid from Freddie unless his arm, tighter round my shoulder as we waited for the street lights to change, could be counted. We reached the entrance to the subway.

"We never did make the art galleries," he said.

"I suppose I could come back in spring."

"Why don't you?"

"Why should I?"

We were threading among crowds in the ticket hall.

"If you could manage April I would be free then."

He held onto my arm, shoulder, waist or shirt, wherever he could as I paid my fare and made for the barrier.

"Right Freddie. April it is. I'll probably write first when I'm back in Britannia Village."

"I'll try not to reply in economic equations. Tell me, what's Gerry going to think?"

"Much the same as your married women, I'd guess. Something for all of us to work on. There's nothing much for him to think, is there?"

On the far side of the barrier I was caught up in a swirl of print-workers and late-night waiters making for the western suburbs. I thought I'd said goodbye then recollected I'd overlooked Freddie's Englishness – or was it my own? I looked back. He hadn't moved. There he was, grinning: my downfall, my cricket captain, my recurrent dream and my despair. He waved shyly until I'd shouldered my way back.

"Freddie Clay. We're both too old and plain-spoken to be rerunning spotty old films like Les Enfants du Paradis and Brief Bloody Encounter. Fuck off home will you? I'll be here in April."

"I'll have tidied the apartment .."

"Big deal. Do I call for tea and toast?"

Freddie frowned more deeply than before. The smile in his eyes broke into fragments of blue glass. His voice was a dry whisper.

"Won't you be coming to stay?"

"Well, I for one am not into a repeat of this evening, getting high on moonlight and sore balls. That's for sure. Don't blush. One more thing ... will those two cops beat us up if I kiss you here?"

His fingers gripped the barrier so fiercely that there was little blood in them. He looked directly at me and it was as deadly as the missile I'd been dodging for years. His mouth opened and his jaw worked as though, recovering from a knock-out blow, he was battling to speak.

"Not here ... at home ... why not at home? Please."

"I'll fall asleep with jet lag."

"Doesn't matter. Please ... can I help you over the barrier?"

"If you don't stand back, I may kick you in the teeth."

Like swimming, like loving, gate-vaulting is a knack never forgotten. I was over and we kissed our way out of the station without the cops giving us a second glance.

PETER ROBINS
Trilogy: *II. Second Best*

Gerry swung his arm through an arc from my thigh to the carpet, scrabbling there on what I still thought of as his side of the divan.

"Twenty past one?" I suggested between nibbling the hollow of his shoulder.

"Two minutes out."

Eyes still screwed from squinting at the digits, he kissed me, disengaged himself, shuffled pillows, finally propped both head and torso against them. I pushed my tongue casually round his navel rim in a movement that pleased us.

"Was it better than New York or not as good?"

What chance did he suppose he had of throwing me? When you've shared it – everything – five full years, it's a rare routine that floors you. Home from assignments in Oslo, Rome, Algiers I'd learned to expect artless probing. This time the challenge lacked preamble yet I knew it must come. As Gerry waited I realised there'd been too many anecdotes about the tourist spots; too few references to Freddie.

"Sounds like an optician testing for myopia," I made the tone light as I could, abandoned his navel, pumped my own pillows so we were facing in the greyness. Best, I'd decided in the homebound plane, to say what had to be said after our first reunion. No dodging. I ought to have calculated Gerry might feel the same.

"So ... was it?"

"As good in a different way."

He lit cigarettes for us, eased an arm round my shoulder. I was forecasting his next ploy, used so often when there'd been nothing to tell. Gerry's compulsive need to balance our ledger.

His casual infidelities never cost me an hour's sleep. Weekends at the coast with Sue, then Wendy, I'd let pass. Not being over-possessive, I'd not questioned conflicting details of occasional business conferences. An extra-affectionate Sunday night had been explanation and apology.

"I've told you before" – I was silently pacing each phrase – "I'd not object if you did go to bed with him." Objection irrelevant, the case is altered. "It would keep it in the family almost ..."

"You're three jumps ahead. Who says we went to bed? Ever thought being with him might have been ..."

"I know you" – exhaling, he bit my neck lightly – "As I said: makes no difference."

"Sure?"

"Positive."

It probably didn't for Gerry. He sped easily through strange bedrooms, maybe always would, not intending to hurt. Half of him hungered for steady affection; the other chafed at the routine, demanding the occasional change of bedscape. That had been no reason for our break-up.

"But this is different?"

"You mean the colour scheme? Well now Gerry, you've not been round for ..."

"Not the bloody walls and you know it. Green was never my special thing though ..."

Could he think I had sat pining? Kept the place as we'd once planned? I anticipated a question about freshening the room for Freddie's London visit. Had asked myself each dozen brush strokes. Too easy. It was the room as I wanted it back from my first long holiday for years.

"No idea if Freddie goes for green, so don't ask."

"Stop playing, thickhead. Freddie's different from the Toms, Dicks and Harries who've been here since we split. Right?"

Gerry raised his brows, wrinkled his forehead. Eyes twinkled at me through shadow and he squeezed my bicep. His laugh, as I winced, had fear at the core. I saw a man searching some toehold as he tumbled.

"Freddie wasn't a cheap pad or an easy fuck, if that's what you're on to. He's not, repeat not, Tom, Dick or Harry."

"I should never have moved out." I knew that sigh. He was brushing down a costume for one of his roles. "This need never have happened. We could have done the States together. Might have been fun meeting him again – with you."

"Stop fantasising. You've been out of sixth form ten years ..."

"I mean it." He filled my glass, nibbled my ear lobe, then emptied down the bottle with a gurgle and belched. "I'm serious. You know, I feel like leaping out of bed this instant, drawing a grand I haven't got. We could piss off somewhere. South America might do: sunshine, just us and no one hassling me. You've never leaned on me. One reason I still love you."

"Remind me to get you a check shirt and straw hat for your wedding day, Huck Finn."

"You rotten shit."

"Cheers."

It was shock therapy when Gerry got high on romanticism. I'd weathered his joining the army reserve to strut the neighbour-hood in a catchy uniform. Friends asked if I'd gone kinky or Gerry had managed to deceive himself. I'd waited two years and the gear was shoved to the back of a cupboard among soccer boots and yachting cap. I'd coped with Gerry's tearful last exit: the half coherent line that women were beginning to mean more. Not that Deirdre had ever been pregnant. All the characters in Gerry's repertoire were suddenly fuzzy like snaps in a stranger's family album. Why shelter him from the cool light of here and now?

I finished the Soave with a gulp.

"On the belt Gerry, old love, but not under. Yes, you'll love me but I'll have to slot in – maybe Deirdre too? – with the heavy calls of suburban respectability – yes? How the hell do you square being one month from the Wedding March with snuggling against me now?"

Fingers locked round my neck. His lips, tongue, nose were trying to rouse me. I tugged gently until he was lying over me, our eyes not six inches apart.

"We haven't got time ..."

"Trust me" – tears were starting and Gerry's no West End actor – "It'll be like this when I'm married, she won't even begin to guess. Deirdre's very naive. I don't want to hurt her. Or you. Listen. It won't affect loving her if I pop round. This doesn't damage my relationship with Deirdre ..."

"Or mine with Freddie?"

His body arched, rested on one elbow and a finger stubbed between my ribs. Twice.

"So you do love him?"

"Watch it, Sherlock. It's not a game. People bleed and cry."

The let-down had to be easy for our breakup hadn't curdled affection. Yet it had to be plain Freddie was no holiday high. With him, I'd rediscovered dimensions Gerry and I had forgotten.

Relaxed honesty. No convention ruling out a hundred topics, until the realisation that I'd contracted for a part not in a relationship, but a stylised parody.

"Gerry love. I mean love. Sometimes, on a bus say, or at a party, I sense I'm one step outside the action. There's just one litmus test then: who do I wish was there to share the quiet joke ...?"

"Answer?"

"Has to be Freddie."

I lit cigarettes, aware we were smoking too much, lost for any other anaesthetic.

"So everything we shared goes in the waste bin? Being penniless together in Scotland? Moving-in day?"

"Yes, that's great for reminiscing by the fire but, Gerry, we're not building any more."

Heaving himself from me he was sitting up, about to hit out. Pride must be restored.

"For Christ's sake. You're fifty. What's this new horizons drill? Can't you be content with me? Or maybe Freddie's sex-charge at thirty-five's low enough not to exhaust your autumn years?"

"Stop feeling slighted. Maybe it's my romanticism respond-ing to wider horizons than we've been offering each other. Anyway, in autumn humanists don't defer fun on the offchance. I've always asked the best of myself, Gerry, now I'm going to have just that for myself ..."

"Meaning Freddie, not me. Why don't you fuck off to New York?"

It was my own waking question. No more hazardous a chance than the other I was taking. Cautious as ever, remember-ing too many foundered affairs, I was content to monitor first the way things went, with two flights a year for each of us over the herring pond. The first arrangement in six years of no concern to Gerry.

"Emigrate? Nice dream like your overdrawn grand. But I've got a mortgage like you've got a marriage ..."

"So, while Mr Marvellous is in the States, I'll do?"

"And when you've rowed with Deirdre?"

I knew that manic swing out of bed, wondered if it was to be silence, a banged street door, snuffled apologies from a call box on the Embankment at some barbaric hour. Gerry tugged on shirt and socks before turning to kiss me.

"I do love you, for Christ's sake I do. That makes you a first class citizen among those making do. And you know you fucking

love me. That makes us supercitizens. How can you chuck it up
for someone who's a possibility three bloody thousand miles
away?"

I reached my hand to cup his scrotum, kissed his penis from
dark puckered foreskin to first hair matted with sweat and tacky
sperm. Rolling over, I pulled his face down.

"D'you think I'd do this for some flouncy chorus boy? Mind
you, he does have a snub nose. Anyway," I delved to grab his
watch, "ten to two. More files for you and a skirting board for
me."

"Will he stay here? In our bed?"

"Put the violin down, will you, and start sprinting."

By the street door he offered another cigarette. I refused.
Having peeled back my dressing-gown, he squeezed me to him.

"Next Monday ok if I bring ...?"

"The Soave?"

"You'll be here?"

"I don't plan to sell the home."

"You see? That's what I like. The sense of coming home."

"You read too many bad novels on the bus."

"Be serious. Are we making use of each other?"

I kissed the dimple in his chin. Gerry liked that.

"No amount of talking can scrub out Freddie ... or Deirdre.
You've got six minutes. Scoot."

I watched the window for ten seconds until Gerry put his
head over the garden wall and did his Pinocchio grin. Another ten
seconds and I walked to the phone. Breakfast time in New York.

PETER ROBINS
Trilogy: *III. Second Hand*

Gerry has told me since then that it was close on ten before they
wondered if I would show. My estimate that they'd have sufficient
to catch up on to keep them chatting for a couple of hours hadn't
been so far out. If I was one common link between them, it was a
reasonable bet Freddie wouldn't explore it overmuch. There
were a dozen others beginning with staff, former pupils and
subsequent careers. Gerry would have recognised his form
master as readily as I'd done in New York. Whether Freddie
would have known the reformed skinhead had he not called from
the hotel lobby is questionable, but there they sat from eight till
ten in Freddie's room, looking back on a sixth-former in a blazer
and a young teacher fresh from Cambridge. From all I'd heard it
had been a very average suburban school, but rich enough in
anecdote for the two of them to reminisce their way down half a
bottle of gin.

"Freddie wasn't exactly tickled," Gerry told me, "when I
checked my watch and suggested you'd set us up so I'd lose my
train and we'd complete the triangle by hopping into bed."

He wouldn't have been. Freddie's English romanticism has
survived five years in the Big Apple. I could still hear his accent,
his turn of phrase, finicky in argument as Cambridge folk often
are, echoing in Christopher Street. In a brief panning shot I
recalled his apartment bulging with early editions that almost
distracted from those photographs.

Gerry, by contrast, has always been earthy and robust –
capable of murmuring as a bus slows down, "Is there time to nip
home and fuck?" He was just about to say just that the other
lunchtime, though I'd gone through three pints underlining yet

again that the terms on which we meet have altered. Still likes to make the running, does Gerry, as he did ten years back when I stood him a half on his first venture to a gay bar with the imprint of a prefect's cap scarcely faded from his forehead. Within ten minutes he'd asked if it was far to my place. Wasn't difficult to guess his inexperience, but we'd been seeing each other a full month before I knew he wasn't twenty-one and had been a virgin.

When Tessa asked if I could point to one essential difference between them it had to be that Freddie knows precisely what he wants in his career but not in his personal relationships, but with Gerry it's vice versa. Having married Deidre, set himself up with a winterweight suit and a millstone of a mortgage, Gerry winks in his shaving mirror at the respectable commuter who eluded him when we lived together. He remains very nippy on the footwork when there's any question of image preservation. Wouldn't falter at the open door of a gay bar if a queue welcomed him with knickers round their ankles. No cruising the station cottages at rush hour for him either. It's me or no one. Arrogance? No – just that Gerry has no male friends and chooses to channel all mateship and affection on me.

We recalled our first encounter one Monday lunchtime when I was planning my States visit. He could hardly question who I might bed. I mentioned calling on Freddie. When I gave him the surname Gerry supplied height, weight, colouring and age. I wouldn't go as far as Tessa, who contends there are only two hundred gays in the whole country, the rest being a clones and mirrors job. It was a smile, though, that Freddie had been Gerry's form master. I should have noted that Gerry, unhappy at the possibility of needing to share me as person, had already drawn me about the one weekend I'd had with Freddie. For the ten minutes before we were both randy again, we worked on the possibility that I'd first seduced Gerry on Friday, skipped the launderette through lack of time next day, and had Freddie on the same stained sheets after a Saturday party.

"Will you tell Freddie that?"

"Not if he's as prim about sex as he was then ..."

He was and I hadn't, but Gerry had after they'd been nattering for more than an hour. Freddie, it seems, went all terse and Senior Common Room and said what went on in private bedrooms was the concern of the two participants. There was a light stress on the word "two", Gerry giggled. Then Freddie had made huffily for the bathroom. That detail sounded likely but I felt bound by some affection to defend him.

"Well, that's his code. You wouldn't be giggling if I slipped along to the Antenatal to let Deidre know you nip over at lunch break because you're pissed off with wrist jobs ..."

That was only updating what I'd told him privately at his Stag Night. Either our relationship develops or dies. Sex for sentiment's sake is out.

Freddie's sentimentality is different. He goes for perfection: unflawed looks and a Mensa mind. His tentative affairs with women in New York founder because each falls short on one score chart or the other. I told him why at a stand-up breakfast bar. Three photographs on the inside of a cupboard door gave the answer. It's eighteen-year-olds. Sixth-form heroes when he was prepubescent. Others he'd lusted for at the next desk as he'd revised for university entrance. Could be some who'd been in Gerry's class but weren't skinheads. Freddie was adamant they were merely milestones of innocent friendship. But he blushed.

Home from New York I'd accepted for some weeks Freddie was too pushed to write or phone regularly. Calling him one Monday with Gerry's aftershave still spicing the back of my hand, I first detected a wariness. Finally he scrawled a dozen lines, letting me know he'd ring as soon as he was in London. There was the impression throughout that afternoon and often later (though pride prevented any discussion with Gerry) that Freddie was struggling to push me into a containable space in his timetable. The news wasn't too devastating when he did phone, two days after arrival. His hotel was a mile from home.

"Fine," I said, "eight o'clock tomorrow. I expect Gerry can make it."

Then I cycled over to see Tessa. When she'd heard it all, she just shrugged.

"So where's the problem? Stop fretting about their romanticism and think of your own. It's not how far they'll allow you into their bloody lives, but how you slot them into yours."

It's good to have somebody on the outside who's cool and can coax you into laughing at yourself. We were on our third coffee when Tessa suggested going with me to the hotel. She's worked in the next office for three years and is the most together lesbian I've ever met. Hates labels and categories and sees sex as an expression of affection wherever it's offered and reciprocated. Maybe because, like Gerry, she's immediate and outgoing, she took to him quickly. Just as well, since he didn't hang about after we'd stumbled along the hotel corridor more than a bit pissed at ten-thirty. There was chit-chat while Gerry finished his gin, but I knew he was assessing how far Tessa might threaten his standing with me. His tone was too light and bantering when he left to scoot for his train and I wondered how long it might be before he phoned me.

Freddie had become gauche and formal. The jet lag hadn't been too foul. The hotel wasn't over-expensive and usefully central. Two hours in a bar with Tessa had relaxed me, so I was amused, not in a vindictive way, by Freddie's bewilderment. Tessa flicked my ear as she wandered to the bathroom.

Freddie wondered why I had brought her.

"Because I'm through with being your London newsletter, Freddie. Sick of fondling your trendy interest in fringe politics and gay thinking and any other of the few ideas still alive on this island. I wanted you, but I endangered your carefully constructed lifestyle."

No answer to that question. I was more pissed than I had thought.

"No. What I really mean is I'm less predictable than you supposed. That's a threat too, isn't it? Tessa's not here as my entrance badge to the bisexual club. We might sleep together tonight but then again she could be into Martians this week ..."

"I'm sorry if I've upset you. I had hoped you might be staying overnight ..."

"Had you just? Then what was wrong with my fucking place from the start? Or is it tonight you just don't happen to have any meetings, conferences or relatives on your timetable? When you checked in here, you were saying to me New York was a pleasant reunion but I mustn't interrupt your career. Finish. So I'm on my own. You can forget April, Freddie, even if you've not thought better of it anyway. Tessa ... you having a bath?"

We didn't linger. Freddie was dithering and frowning. What else should one expect of the English academic when confronted with distasteful emotion? His one letter was a faultless elaboration of the cliché that we should be good friends and play it from there. It seemed worth one call to try reasoning – and cold, sober argument – but when I cornered him, down went that phone.

Gerry was elated when I saw him a week later. He'd called Freddie the following morning, ostensibly to swop addresses. Having checked I'd not stayed over, he'd concentrated on Tessa's involvement with me. I kept him guessing. Transparent stage manager that he is, it wasn't long before he was proposing I could do worse than marry her. Didn't catch on quickly either, when I said I was sure she'd be delighted and we could always

leave our wives at home knitting while we buddied off to the hills
for weekends.

As we came out of the bar, snow touched and melted on our
faces. Before Gerry could say it, I told him there wasn't time to nip
back to the bedroom.

"Then what about next Monday?"

Gerry tends to selective amnesia when any argument has
gone against him.

"Fine. What d'you want for supper?"

"Difficult. I meant lunchtime ..."

"And I meant supper or nothing. You choose. Be there by
seven, or I'm out."

PAUL MANN
The Park-Job

I first met Sonny in September when there were a few days of summer left; I was sitting on a bench in the park. Sonny knew, with his prostitute's instinct, why I was there. He came over.

He said to me, indicating to the car park: "This bloke over there has an Alfa Romeo ... You got a place?" His accent was of the London area.

I nodded.

"We'll all go to your place then," he said flatly.

I shook my head. And saying no more he left. I mused about the "threesome" with an unseen partner. I thought of Number Three as someone not yet middle-aged but balding, perhaps a beard, tending to be overweight, a man who might need the reassurance of an expensive imported car. Nowadays, now I know Sonny better, I am sure he made the suggestion thinking of collecting a double fee.

The coming winter was long and depressingly cold; the frequenters of the park stayed indoors, or maybe they went to visit pubs – I didn't care. I spent my days writing.

When spring came, I saw Sonny in the High Street; he stared me in the eyes and hesitantly walked by. It seemed to be fate for I saw him the following morning and again in the afternoon; and each time we stared at each other. It was after six that evening, when the traffic thins and people have returned home from work; I walked along the river-bank road towards the park, certain that he would be waiting for me. I followed him into the toilet and stood at one of the sinks. I could hear him behind me noisily shredding paper to attract my attention. I turned and the way he overtly advertised his intention made me gasp.

Back in my house I asked him why he had the sleeves of his

sweater rolled up on such a chilly evening.

"Tough, ain't I?" he replied. I hadn't for a long time seen legs so hairless and white, and feet so long and bony, the soles of which were pitted with athlete's foot. "Fucking footballer's feet, ain't they?" he grinned, agreeing with me when I mentioned how unattractive they were. When I commented on his legs, he looked at them as if examining them objectively for the first time; he said: "Fucking horrible, ain't they?" I gave him "money for the pictures" that day and when he left I thought about him.

The next lunchtime I went to the Dog and Partridge pub and there he was playing darts. He signalled with his eyes that we should meet outside. He came home with me. He carried with him a cheap, gilt statuette he had won playing darts; his name was engraved on a small plate on its base. He set it down proudly next to my record turntable, then he studied the room, asking me how much various objects were worth, and he bet me that the paintings were valuable; he examined a silk screen, then he fingered a heavy silver rose bowl I'd won several years ago when I was a boxer. I had the feeling I was in the company of a cat burglar, a small, juvenile cat burglar casing the joint. He picked up a newspaper and pointed at the photograph of a rather plain society woman. "I'd screw that old cow for *her* money," he remarked simply.

In bed Sonny was obliging. I found something refreshing in the manner he practised his trade.

I discovered he had crabs. He refused to go to the doctor. "I'd rather die of them first," he told me somewhat over-dramatically. I wrote on a slip of paper: "Can I have some ointment for crab lice, please?" and took it into a small chemist shop off the High Street hoping to be served by the man who owned the shop. Unfortunately he was out back. The female assistant's face registered no expression when she read my note.

Sonny returned home two hours later, his breath smelt of beer. He watched fascinatedly. "Fucking horrible things, ain't they? Waving their arms. That ointment fucking stinks."

"Didn't you know you had them?" I asked.

"No. I never looked that close."

"Didn't they itch?"

"Yeah. Something itched. But, Christ, ain't they horrible? ... By the way, I've been thinking about coming to stay here with you. Leaving home. I stole some money off my Dad. I picked his pocket after he had his wage packet. I took five. Fucking kill me he will."

I told him calmly I had no intention that he should live here. I gave him the money.

The next night he arrived after walking back from a pub seven miles away. "I would never ask any of my mates for a lift. They all got cars. I wouldn't never ask any of them."

"Why not try and get a job?" I suggested.

"Yeah! Fucking easy to say it, ain't it? I tell you I tried again and again to get on the site at Lodge Road. I go there every Monday when they take on brickies' labourers. I want that job. But some bastard told the foreman I nick stuff. Bastard! I really want that job." He talked on enthusiastically about it, as some might talk of the excitement of going abroad for a holiday or winning a lot of money at a horse-race meeting. "That's all I want. A job like my mates."

Later he had a bath and we talked until the early hours of the following morning. I teased him when he boasted of his good looks and how he was considered to be very sexy. He grew bolder with familiarity and in reply to one of my questions told me: "You ask a load of shit." Then later: "Christ, you talk a load of fucking shit."

He carried with him at all times a gramophone disc; it was Elvis - *Hound Dog*. He played it over and over again on my turntable, liking the sound reproduction on my equipment.

"I cried when Elvis died," he told me.

He talked, telling me stories of his sexual experiences. "Went to the pictures with this bird and she got my cock out. We was in the back row. And we was watching this sex film where the woman was having it *both* ways in a chair lift going up a fucking mountain. Christ, I shot off so high it landed on this geezer's jacket in front of me. We laughed our cocks off. That wanker sat there with it on his coat all through the film, didn't he?"

The next day - no, I think two days elapsed - he came round and this time he had lost money when he had been out shopping for his Dad and he didn't dare go back because his Dad would kill him. I suggested sensibly that I would give him a certain sum each week rather than have him going to the bother of inventing these financial disasters.

"I ain't lying. You can ask my Dad," he said indignantly.

When I asked him where he lived, he hesitated and was evasive; instead he replied that he agreed to my terms. He didn't haggle but did mention that he had earned ten times that sum in two hours in the West End. I made one condition and that was I didn't want him hanging around the park.

He was affronted: "I swear to you that I don't bother with no men now. Only birds now."

"It isn't that," I said. "It's a stinking place. I don't want you going to the park toilet and picking up a disease and giving it to me."

"I swear to you that I don't bother with *no* men now. I don't bother with no men at all. I swear to you that."

I didn't want to see him too often and we agreed that he should visit Tuesdays and Fridays – Thursdays were his disco nights; Saturdays and Sundays he played pool or darts.

Sunday evening. And I felt tired after writing for too long. I went out to the Dog and Partridge for a drink just before closing time. Sonny was there drinking with an effeminate, weak-chinned male. Sonny saw me at the far end of the bar; he looked frightened. He had been caught out in a lie. But Sonny didn't know I wouldn't be jealous – particularly as the "other man" was a sad specimen and I had made no condition that he shouldn't see other men. But I *was* irritated with his stupid lies. Also, I'll admit, I was fascinated by him because now he was a character in my novel – *my* character. I decided to play a game and to stare at him continuously. After five minutes he came over, furtively glancing from side to side, and in the noisy confusion of people getting in last drinks, he shouted he would come and see me tomorrow. I didn't speak. When the pub shut, I followed him and the man outside and I leant against a wall watching them. They were both very much ill at ease; they glanced back at me apprehensively. The man got into a car and started the engine; Sonny clambered in the passenger seat. I think the car was an Alfa Romeo – but could not be sure.

Next evening he had his finger on the bell-push and left it there. I wasn't annoyed, slightly amused at his aggressive ringing. I gave him five minutes and then I opened the door; his face was red and his light chestnut hair blown wild by the wind. He rushed inside as he always did and sat in a chair biting his nails.

"You've got dandruff," I remarked casually.

"Yeah. Fucking crabs, fucking foot-rot and fucking dandruff. You really got me into the shit last night with my uncle wondering who the fuck you was."

I laughed. "Your *uncle*?"

He bit a thumb nail, desperately pushing the thumb into his mouth, searching for a fragment of nail he might have just possibly missed. I pulled his hand away. The nails were chewed halfway down, the fingers unpleasantly wet. I had stopped laughing at him. He was very nervous, he pushed his other hand into his mouth. He was like a child – sucking.

"Yeah, my fucking uncle. Ok? He owns five shops." He mentioned the shops as though they clinched his story and made it authentic. He added: "I swear to that. I can tell you he wondered what kind of nut you fucking was. You was lucky 'cos I stopped him punching you in the face."

"Yes," I said quietly.

Sonny said: "Always acting – you. Examining me. Playing your fancy questioning with me. Talking shit. All the time shit ... And you knew I'd fucking come here tonight, didn't you? You knew I would come here 'cos I left that statue here, didn't I? That's worth money, that is."

He knew that the worst was over and that I wouldn't cause trouble. He stood up and went through a door at the end of the room into a cloakroom; he returned drying his hands. He threw the towel back into the cloakroom as though it were a cricket ball, then he crossed to his cheap statuette and re-positioned it.

He said to me: "Get some beers out of the fridge and I'll play Elvis."

I shook my head.

"You get some food then? I haven't eaten all day. Same like those sandwiches I had the other night. And I don't want that margarine crap on the bread, neither."

I took no notice and switched on the remote control unit for the television. Sonny tried another tactic, now he started to play the role of the tempter. He undid his fly and started to play with himself.

"You often do that, do you?" I asked, disinterestedly.

"Yeah. All the time, don't I? At home all the fucking time with my Dad and my little sister watching television ... You are a cunt, Eddie."

It was the first time he had used my name. His tone was amused, the expletive was an endearment; he was showing affection. He did up his trousers. I reached for the control unit and flicked over channels.

He shouted: "Leave it! That's football coming on now! Turn it back!"

I flicked it back and mentioned: "I did want to watch a particular programme on the other side."

"That is ok as it is now. Leave it." He didn't chew his nails at all right through the first half of the game.

During the commercials, he said: "I *almost* broke my word

to you, Eddie, I went to do a park-job today."

"Oh yes."

"Two offers I got in ten minutes. I am telling you this and not one word of a lie. Two offers." He waited. I made no comment so he explained: "You know. To do it to me. Ten quid each to fuck me – nothing else." Sonny looked very pious and pleased with himself as he added: "I said, No. I said to myself no one is ever going to do that to me again – only Eddie if he wants. I said that."

"Can I switch over to my programme now?"

"No, for fuck's sake! It's only half fucking time!"

A woman on the screen was extolling the virtues of her detergent and how right it was for her, no other powder could ever do; an aggressive and irritating woman, as she was intended to be. Sonny wouldn't know that I had set up that commercial.

"How'd you get started on this park-job business?" I asked.

"Well, I'm handsome. Women and men find me very attractive. Funny, isn't it? Sexy. And I'm a neat dancer too."

"The park-jobs, Sonny!"

"Ok. I'm coming to them, ain't I? I went into the bog there for a crap and someone had taken out a brick in the wall. It was a fucking big hole – not a little one and I saw through the hole these two geezers jacking each other off. That was two years ago when I was fifteen. I didn't know about men doing it together then. I shouted through the hole that I would do it for them for a fag and they gave me two quid each."

Sonny's attention was being drawn back to the television; the teams were coming out onto the pitch.

"You don't enjoy sex with men much at all, do you?"

"You know every fucking thing, don't you? I'm young, ain't I? I likes women, don't I? You know all about me, don't you? That fucking bog stinks. I am really telling you the truth now, Eddie. Christ, I hate it waiting for hours in the stinking cold in there."

He was watching the players take up their positions – I was running out of conversation-time allowed. I took hold of his arm – Sonny always accepted physical contact; to him my touching him was a natural thing for me to do. I pointed out the tattoo, a crudely inscribed DAD. I asked where he had had it done.

"That? I did it myself with Indian ink and a needle ..." Then the anaesthetic was taking hold, he was slipping, he was gone, immersed in the match. I examined his fresh face, his fine curling hair, the cheap red and white check shirt torn below the pocket which held a black comb with greasy dirt between the teeth; the cardigan had three buttons missing; the fashion pants were thin and threaded at the cuffs. He had his shoes off and I could smell his socks. He liked to boast to me how his feet stank and how he'd had crab lice: it was as though they were campaign medals, in a curious way lending him virility.

I left him there and went down to the pub where I drank a pint and bought a dozen beers to take out. When I returned the match had finished and Sonny had drunk the remaining beers in the fridge. He took one of the cans I had brought back from the pub and complained it was not chilled enough.

What Sonny didn't realise was that he had finished the part he played in my book; he had taken up, I admit, more pages than I had previously thought. My characterisation was complete and now the necessity of Sonny was finished.

I listened to him chatting happily, tilting his head back to laugh as he drank more and more beer. Then he leant forward and shook my arm. "Didn't pinch nothing from you when you were out, did I? I told you before I wouldn't. I got this suspended sentence for shop-lifting. I wouldn't dare touch nothing now. My Dad almost killed me then. But he paid the fine and that shit. And he had me back after the detention centre."

Always his Dad, always his Dad. I assumed but I didn't ask him then, that his Mother had left home. I put some money into his pocket – far more than the modest rates we had agreed on – and told him quietly it was over. He had not expected it.

He shouted: "You bastard! I'll tell the police. I'll tell them I knocked on your door to ask for a glass of water and you forced me to do terrible things."

I grinned at him.

"You bastard," he said. "You know I fucking wouldn't, don't you? Can't, can I? I don't honestly understand you, Eddie, because we both likes each other. I knows what you done is fair. It's ok, that what we agreed, and you said either of us could stop it when we wanted. You given me enough money?"

I nodded. He didn't bother to check it.

He said: "Ok, Eddie, this is it. It's over. You'll never see me again. Not now. I never go down that stinking hole again neither."

It was odd that he shook hands. I thought afterwards how strange that was. I sat thinking after he had gone, looking at the scattered empty beer cans.

In my story, Sonny had blackmailed a man and the man was more vengeful than frightened. The man went to the local town hall and, remembering the surname engraved on the base of the gilt statuette, traced the youth's address by going through every street in the voting list. It was an unusual surname – Sonny had no mother. I looked now at the trophy by the record turntable; originally he had even told me that it was stolen, then he had changed his story. "It's mine. I wouldn't steal nothing now I'm going straight." I had read several of the many letters he had received from admiring girl friends on holiday here – he was careful never to allow me to read the address on the envelopes – one in a large round hand told him how much she loved him and she was going to have a baby and only wanted him more and more. In my story, the man steals a page of the letter and imitates the girl's handwriting and writes to Sonny's Dad, telling him the truth about Sonny and his male prostitution. To mail his letter the man drives to the girl's home town – one hundred and forty miles north – thus ensuring the postmark was correct. A cruel, vindictive man. Mind you, he was being blackmailed.

But in real life, to be blackmailed by Sonny? Never. It would involve too much effort. I remember when I discovered about his crab lice and we had both gone out that same afternoon: me to the chemists and he to meet a girl. On return, he told me: "Even you could have screwed it." She gave him drinks then she asked him for it. I had asked: "For what? You mean for you to have sex with her?" He had nodded impatiently. When I protested to him, reminding him of his crab lice and the probability of transferring them to her, he thought for a while, then, as if to make his sleeping with her acceptable to me, said: "I kept me trousers on, didn't I? I just stuck it out through the fly."

I knew that Sonny was scared of his Dad and me. Both of us cared for him and he knew it. I liked his inept lies and his guttersnipe charm.

It was a week after the "final" parting, I saw him cross my front lawn from the path by the river. His face peered in through the window, searching for me beyond the privacy of the net curtain. I let him in. He rushed in with his head down. He sat and talked pleasantries for an hour. Then he explained he was expecting some money – a cheque which should have arrived yesterday but hadn't and as he hadn't eaten, could I lend him a few quid? *Lend* he stressed. He wasn't, he explained, begging, and he knew precisely how much money he had borrowed before. He assured me – despite my protests – that the money I had given him when he picked his Dad's pockets and had dropped that shopping money could only be treated by him as borrowing. But his heart wasn't really in his explanations. The game had palled a little. He looked at the table where I kept the telephone and some loose change in case anyone came to the door begging for a charity, and he jumped up nodding at the money. I let him take the coins.

He said: "I promise this, Eddie. I will pay back the money I mentioned. I tell you this, I will come back later tonight and I'll give you the best fucking night you've ever had *anywhere* in your fucking life. I'll do everything for you."

Two days later I'd been to the bank and walked home via the park. Sonny was back outside his money-yielding toilet; he was talking to a man with a black moustache – ten years younger than me, I would guess. I would have thought that Sonny would have pretended not to see me. I was wrong. He winked, I felt the excitement of an accomplice. He immediately left the man and came over.

"I'm in the shit again," he said. He zip-fastened his red wind-breaker, then added: "I've been thinking."

"Oh yes?"

We walked out of the park gates onto the river road, avoiding the parked cars of early summer visitors.

"That bloke with the moustache said you were tough-looking – handsome." Then, as though he had fouled up his attempted flattery, added: "And young."

"I'm forty. Forty-one next month."

"Forty is nothing at all. And now I got to come back with you to get my statue I won for playing darts. It's worth cash that."

"It's a very valuable trophy," I teased.

"You pulling my fucking pisser?"

"Yes."

"I'll come back and get it now." He hesitated, not looking at me, not probably expecting an answer: 'Ok then to come?"

We were walking by the bus stop; an attractive girl stood there alone.

"Christ!" swore Sonny. "Look at that, Eddie. Look at the fucking knockers on it!"

As we passed he turned to stare at her. "Shaft that! I bet you anything you like I could." He walked backwards looking at her. He said to me when she was out of sight: "I'll come back to your place and stay three hours. It's Thursday night and that."

"Do you really reckon you could have made it with that girl?"

He laughed. "No fucking chance. No chance there."

I teased him: "What about your looks?"

"Pah! What looks, you cunt?"

I said: "I've remembered now. Thursday night is disco night."

"Yeah ... and I want to be straight with you, Eddie. Don't get me wrong 'cos the way I did it the other night was for free and that. I just want enough money to get into the disco – that's all. And for one or two drinks. Stop grinning, you bastard. For Christ's sake, you got me chewing me fingers. My fuck awful nerves! My nerves are fuck awful. I swear that I wasn't there to do a park-job. Him with the moustache you saw – that's Rod – you and him are the only men I've allowed to be intimate with me that way."

"Intimate with ... " I repeated, amused at his use of language.

"Yeah!" he shouted loudly. "Intimate with, and that's the fucking truth!"

He saw the expression on the face of a woman pedestrian who overheard and after she was out of earshot, he said to me:

"You know what I think of her, don't you?"

I nodded and said: "Yes, Sonny, I know and I don't want to hear it."

He did a little dance to show he was a footballer, then started to shadow box at the air, then at me, feigning punches to my face and body. Then he ran ahead to the house dribbling a stone, kicking it with his plastic shoes.

He found the side door unlocked and he went in and before I reached the path I could hear Elvis. He knew he didn't have to ask me if he could use the record-player now.

He sat smiling, relaxed, talking to me, drinking and listening to the Elvis record over and over again. I didn't tell him I had checked his address on the voter's list at the town hall and then had later visited a pub near his home and the publican had told me his father had died just one year ago.

When it was time for Sonny to leave, he casually mentioned he couldn't take the statuette with him this time because he was going straight on to the disco.

"Anyway," he said. "I come here to stay, ain't I?"

I grinned, saying nothing.

"Yeah," he said, knowingly. "You know everything. I'll come back tonight to stay."

Outside on the path he turned and made a grotesque face at me and a V-sign with his fingers. He had left Elvis on the turntable.

Now, when he is told off by me, he shouts at me saying I'm always teasing him, always telling him off. "You're a bastard – just like my fucking Dad was," he says.

DAVID REES
At the Gym

Some time ago I came to the conclusion that I badly needed strenuous physical exercise. The dangerous age, forty-five; angina or cardiac arrest looming on the horizon, my general state of health not assisted by smoking twenty cigarettes a day and the totally sedentary routine of a writer's life. Me, an ash-tray, a chair, a table, a pen, a sheet of paper. Nothing very physical about all that.

I had no alarming symptoms. It was just that I was fed up with always feeling ... well, yucky. So I enrolled at the local gym, my fears of pulled muscles and torn tendons somewhat lessened by the thought of toasting myself on the sunbed and sweating buckets in the sauna. I've always liked saunas. Yes, yes, I *know*, but there was nothing cruisy about this one, nor had I expected, or even wanted, there to be. Straight as a die it was. When I first went there.

It's tempting to write a satirical piece about the gym. All those grunts and groans like second-rate orgasms from fat bank managers, insurance clerks, university lecturers and shop assistants heaving barbells and dumbells all over the place; the stench of male armpits and sweaty jockstraps and unwashed socks; white, middle-aged flesh with bald patches of skin caused by years of the wrong sort of clothes rubbing off body hair; the interminable conversations about diets and weight loss and the best exercise for this or that particular bit of the torso. And the jargon: thigh curls, thigh extensions (not as interesting as they sound), chins, squat-thrusts, leg-raises, side-raises, calf-raises, twist-aways, good-mornings, bench-presses, etcetera, etcetera. It tooks me months to discover what b.o. rowing was – nothing to do with eradicating skin smell – and flat-flying, which sounded extremely athletic, if not highly dangerous, turned out to be a very prosaic few minutes on one's back with a pair of dumbells. There were exercises for every part of the anatomy, except one. A pity: I'm sure all of us, gay or straight, would have enjoyed practising cock raises and plonker extensions. Enlargement in that particular region would have done wonders for many of the clients, though I have to admit that, in the sauna, I could not help noticing one or two amazing prodigies.

But I don't want to be satirical about the gym. I really enjoyed my three visits a week: the work-out was often utterly exhausting, but after the hour on the sunbed and in the sauna, I felt so alive, so mentally and physically relaxed I was ready for anything. I don't think it's my imagination being too inventive, but the whole quality of life began to improve. I could now settle easily to writing; I slept soundly; and I could dance all night at a disco and not feel the strain. Even sex seemed more exciting and more frequent, though that has a lot to do with Ulrich, who is an insatiable kid and an absolute turn-on. Just thinking about him gives me an erection! As if I was still seventeen. Thanks, solely, to the gym? Probably not, but there's no doubt it helps.

My body's in better shape. I'm getting those biceps I used to envy so much in other men; I can see a line right down my middle from throat to navel, and though I'll never have a stomach like a washboard, it's reasonably flat and firm. I'm not ashamed now to peel off my shirt in the middle of a strenuous bout of disco dancing.

But enough about my body: back to the gym. I began to like the crowd who went there. "All right, then?" they always said in greeting, instead of "Hullo," as if everything was a huge struggle against overwhelming odds. They were a pleasant, easy-going lot, though I didn't make any close friends, no one I wanted to introduce to other areas of my life. They were all so straight. The gym, I rapidly decided, was the one bit of my existence where I dared not come out, particularly as there didn't seem to be any other gay person who was a member.

At first, as I said. I talked in the Hope and Anchor, our gay pub, about my new-found hobby, and some of my friends and acquaintances showed a real interest, gay men being so much more conscious of and concerned for their figures and their clothes than straight men. Not a weakness, not vanity, not even yearning to be ever youthful, as the the world might imagine: looking after the body and dressing well simply make you feel good. Anyway, Martin needed little prompting from me to enrol and, after him, Jack, then Steve. And Paul and Andy and Phil and Roger. And Ulrich.

We all tried our best to be discreet, though Martin required an occasional glare when his eyes popped out on stalks at some delectable chicken languidly turning over in the sauna. The others agreed with me that here camping it up or wearing *Gay Love is the Real Thing* badges or trying to sell the CHE Broadsheet would, to put it mildly, be counter-productive. The straight clientele, though they suspected nothing, must have found some of our circumlocutious chatter bewildering, if not incomprehensible. We always referred to *Gay News* as the *Church Times*, the pub as the Usual Place, and in talk about our lovers or the men we fancied we never employed pronouns or Christian names, so that as well as baffling the hets we ended up at times unable to understand each other. It was excellent practice in the Use of English.

Not all the members of the gym were old and fat; there were some superb specimens of muscular, animal youth. Pete was a dream come true: a perfect body, golden skin, piercing blue eyes and a mop of ash-blond hair. A lazy, arrogant masculinity that some men whose work is physical and out of doors exude: an air of "I can take it or leave it" in reference to every facet of their lives. They invariably sprawl rather than sit, as this boy did in the sauna, legs wide apart, utterly relaxed, big hands idly dangling in front of his nice, thick cock. In bed, you'd feel they would be as slow and lazy at first as they'd be about anything, but when roused, my God, what a superb fuck they would be!

Steve and Martin and Paul and Phil and Jack and Roger and Andy and Ulrich and I often talked about Pete. How well-spent an hour with him would be! Etcetera. He was completely straight, of course.

"I'm not so sure," Martin said.

"Oh he is, he *is*!" said Jack. "A wicked waste!"

The rest of us agreed with Jack. Then Pete started coming to the gym with Norman, who was as weedy, spotty and unattractive as Pete was fit, firm and beautiful.

"What did I tell you?" said Martin, triumphantly.

"They're just friends," I said.

"Loads of guys come here in pairs," said Andy. "They like doing the circuit together. Takes their minds off the pain, I suppose."

"They were talking about boobs just now," said Roger. "*Female* boobs."

"Ugh!" Martin exclaimed in mock horror, and waved his wrists.

"Martin!" we chorused.

"You'll get us all slung out of here one of these days," Roger said.

So much for circumlocutions and lateral thinking! Pete came into the changing-room, gave us a rather peculiar look, and started to undress. I hurried back into the work area, and did twenty more than usually vigorous thigh extensions.

None of us could be persuaded that Martin was right in his diagnosis, but there were odd signs. They often touched. That would mean nothing in any country in the world except Britain, whose straight men, the most untactile creatures in existence, make a positive fetish of avoiding bodily contact in case, presumably, anyone should imagine for half a second that they passionately fuck each other all night long. American males, I notice, are constantly slapping one another's backs or putting an affectionate hand on a friend's elbow, and it signifies nothing homosexual. But Pete was often helping Norman's arm on the last bench-press or side-raise. Absurd that Ulrich and I studiously avoided doing things like that, just in case! And they giggled a lot, or indulged in long, whispered conversations. I began to wonder if they'd realised our interest in Pete, but I dismissed the idea. They'd have to have exceptionally keen ears to know what we were talking about.

One day in the sauna I found myself alone with Pete, and we spoke for the first time. I held my hands between my legs as he did, but not for the same reason: I was afraid of the messages my eyes, when confronted with that beautiful blond body, would send to my brain, and that my brain would order my cock to start having an independent life of its own. Our talk was the usual stuff about the sunbed being the best part of the routine – "Bronzing my buns in the waffle iron" as he put it – and was I entering for the Exeter marathon? Then the subject changed to holidays. He and Norman were going to spend a fortnight in Amsterdam.

"AM-STER-DAM!!" Martin shrieked when I told him. Ulrich, fortunately, shoved his hand over Martin's mouth. When released, he said, "That proves it. That bloody proves it!"

"It proves nothing," said Jack.

"But it does look suspicious," said Roger.

We all decided that it did look suspicious. I was press-ganged into finding out more at the next available opportunity.

Which was, as it happened, very difficult. Not that Pete, now the ice had been broken, was unwilling to chat, but he gave nothing away. I learned various fragments of useless information, such as what beer he preferred, that he was a keen supporter of Exeter City, that he didn't like getting up early in the morning. And I'd been wrong about the out-of-doors labouring: he was a PE student. I returned to the subject of Amsterdam, said I'd been there. Where were he and Norman planning to stay? In a tent, he answered. Oh-ho, I thought: very intimate. "There are some excellent saunas in Amsterdam," I said. That produced no particular reaction. "Are there?" he replied, his voice betraying no curiosity whatsoever.

"He never mentions girls," was the only information I could give to the others.

"Why don't you ask him out for a drink?" Martin suggested.

"What for?"

"So we can know whether he is or isn't, stupid!"

"*You* ask him."

"You're the one he talks to."

"Talking's free. Why don't you talk to him? I'm not all that interested, anyway."

"Oh yes you are!" said Ulrich.

"I'm not!"

"I'm sure you'd like to go to bed with him," Ulrich went on. "*I* would."

"Would you tell me if you did?"

"Of course."

We looked at each other and smiled. I could have kissed him at that moment: my sweet, honest, lovely lover. "And *I'd* tell *you* the truth if I did," I said. "And yes, of course I'd like to! Who wouldn't?"

"We're getting off the point," said Jack. "Even supposing he is gay – and I still have doubts on that score – why on earth should we suppose he'd want to have sex with any of *us*? If he is, he's presumably screwing Norman."

"It's that way round, is it?" Andy asked.

"Hmmm. I fancy so." We discussed that for a while, and, yes, we thought; it was probably that way round. "I think Martin's idea is sensible," Jack said. "Invite him out for a drink. Leave here when he does, a little chat in the street, then say 'Don't you work up a dreadful thirst in the gym! Let's have a beer in the Ship.'"

"Ok," I said. "I'll try anything once. Ulrich?"

"If you're asking permission to screw him," Ulrich said, "you

don't need to. Get on with it, and just fill me in on the details when
you come home."

A fortnight and several conversations later, I found myself in
a quiet corner of the Ship, drinking lager with Peter. It was very
convenient, he said, as far as he was concerned; he was meeting
someone in here in half an hour's time. Norman, I assumed; he
hadn't been at the gym that evening: working late, apparently. We
analysed the weather for ten minutes, very cold for the time of
year. And windy. Extremely windy. You didn't expect that in
April. March, yes, but not April. This is ridiculous, I said to myself.
I looked up from my drink and was rather annoyed to see
Jack and Ulrich and Roger at the bar, grinning all over their faces.
"Your friends," Pete said.
"I know."
"I suppose they'll come over here in a minute." He began to
laugh. Quietly at first, as if he was trying with difficulty to control
himself, then soon without any restraint.
"What's the matter?" I asked crossly. It was getting out of
hand: I had an uneasy feeling I was going to end up as the fall-guy in
this particular incident.
He gasped, then said, "I know exactly what you're up to." I
stared at him. "Don't look so astonished. You oughtn't to be."
"Why?"
"You lot seem to think your conversations are so private!
That no one else understands. I've heard every word of every one
of them, and *I* understand all right!"
"So. You're ... one of us?"
"Abba." He started to sing, " 'I saw myself ... as a concealed
attraction .... ' "
"Are you?"
"It has ... been ... known. Yes."
"Norman?"
"Norman!" He began to laugh again. "Not exactly ... the
type. Or my type. Anyway, he's going out with a girl called – would
you believe it? – Gay."
"I'll believe it. I think I'm ready to believe anything!"
"And would you believe –" he glanced at his watch, "– that
the person I'm waiting for in here is my lover?"
"If you say so. Not someone from the gym?"
"No. Not someone from the gym." His blue eyes smiled, full
of mischief. He was absolutely beautiful, I said to myself for the
hundredth time. The white tee-shirt, the black leather jacket, the

skin-tight jeans, showed him off to perfection. I turned round to
see what the others were doing. Jack and Roger were arguing
about something; Ulrich was looking at me. They were not going
to join us, I was glad to observe. "Which of you do I fancy?" Pete
said, "is presumably what you're all dying to know. And if I fancy
any of you, will I go to bed with you? Martin ... well, he's not bad-
looking, but he's too much of a queen. Roger ... nice guy, but I
can't stand beards. Paul's ok, but he'd do nothing for me. Phil,
Steve and Jack ... definitely not. That leaves Ulrich, Andy ... and
you. Ulrich is your lover and I don't go around messing up other
people's affairs. He's delicious, I grant you that." He grinned. A
long silence. Teasing, teasing. "You ... you're all right, but too old
for me. Which leaves Andy. Yes ... I'd go to bed with Andy. But I
shan't. Because ... " He stood up, and smiled at someone who had
just come in through the door."Because my lover's just arrived."
    A girl. A very good-looking girl.
    "I did say it has been known. I didn't say I'm into that at this
point in time. Look ... no hard feelings?" He touched my hand,
squeezed it. "See you at the gym." He went across to the girl, and
a moment later they both walked out of the pub.

    Ulrich could only see the funny side of it, but I felt angry and
humiliated. "Last time I ever do anything Martin suggests!" I said,
on the way home. I punched the air with my fist.
    "All this tension! I thought the gym was supposed to relax
you. Listen, darling. There's a casserole cooking in the slow oven.
We've half a bottle of wine to finish. And we'll watch TV; there's a
programme about my part of Germany I particularly don't want to
miss. Then bed: you can shut your eyes and switch off the lights."
    "What for?"
    "Imagine I'm Pete. You'd like that? Better still, imagine
you're Pete. That's what you really want: to be him, just for an
hour."
    "Is it?"
    He could be right, I thought. Sexual desire is often the
knowledge that the other guy has something about him you lack:
you can never, of course, have that indefinable quality, but
making love with him is the next best thing. The essence of it, in
such close intimacy, may be transferred to you. It isn't, of course;
that's the sadness, afterwards. Indefinable? I knew what Pete had
got that I lacked. A real, lazy, male arrogance. And youth.
    "Sounds like a recipe for a nice evening," I said.
    It was.

I avoided Pete in the gym as much as I could, without being openly rude. He was a little disappointed that I didn't want to talk any more. Perhaps I was being childish, but he was usually with Norman, and I thought it very likely that Norman had been told: there always seemed to be a hint of mockery in his eyes. Why should I let boys nearly half my age take the piss? I said to myself.

Months later, I was extremely surprised one Tuesday night to find Pete in the Hope and Anchor. I was alone: Ulrich had a cold and didn't want to come out; and none of the gay crowd from the gym was in evidence. I couldn't avoid speaking to him. His girl-friend Judith, the one I'd seen in the Ship, had left him for somebody else. He was rather depressed about it, but his arrival in the Hope could only mean one thing: he was on the hunt, this time for a man.

"I can never understand what it's like to be bisexual," I said. "Do you feel when you're with a girl that you want to be with a boy? And vice versa?"

"No. I don't make – in bed I mean – any distinction between the sexes."

"Weird."

"Quite natural. For me."

"What happens if you get married? You might want men on the side."

"Possibly. I'll have to wait and see, won't I?"

"Anyone in here you fancy?"

He looked round, and said, "I think I've chosen the wrong evening."

"Andy's ... not available now. He has a lover."

"I know."

Hmmm. He's tried there, has he? Interesting Andy didn't say anything.

"Do you still find Ulrich delicious?"

He laughed. "If you must know ... yes."

"I'm ... not averse to ... three in a bed."

The rewards of persistence.

It didn't work, though; not for me. In a threesome somebody almost invariably gets left out. Much of the time I watched him screw my lover. A strange, complex sensation caused in part, no doubt, by the fact that Ulrich and I had never taken another man into our bed before. I felt jealous. And rejected. But the sight of those two utterly desirable men making love: how can anyone be so stupid, so idiotic, as to call such an act disgusting, an indecent offence? I don't think I've ever seen anything quite so erotically and aesthetically beautiful.

No harm was done to my relationship with Ulrich.

It didn't happen a second time. And we told no one about it. We didn't want that bandied around the gym!

The three of us became very good friends.

MICHAEL JAMES
Jack Frost

The front door closed with a muted thud.

"How did it go? I've got some coffee perking, be about three minutes." The voice softened, the eyes followed with lively interest as Paul came into the kitchen. "What happened to you? You look quite transformed."

Paul pulled out a cane chair. He eased himself down onto the raffia seat. There was a far-away look on his face that bordered on the beatific.

"You know," he said, looking into those brown, enquiring eyes. "I've thought about it all week. At last it begins to make sense." He reached into his jacket pocket and took out a crisp lilac envelope. He placed it on the table, idly drawing his fingers over the writing on the front.

"Do you fancy something to eat first?" Brown eyes looked at the envelope under Paul's hand. "How about poached eggs on toast?" His tongue slid over his lower lip. "Some of that strawberry jam from your aunt and finish off the Dundee cake I made?"

"Oh yes, perfect." Paul looked directly into the liquid brown eyes that illuminated the strong face. "You have hit it bang on. I'll tell you about it as you get it ready. The coffee has perked, let's have a cup now. Black, strong and without sugar for me. I need to rinse my mouth out with something bitter." The calm, tender voice held no urgency. He smiled. "It all fell into place when I read this letter. There is another one, more detailed, more formal, but this," he said, circling it with his finger, "this is the most important one."

The smooth flow of words accompanied brown eyes, as he

prepared the coffee with a casual efficiency, his movements
unhurried and sure. A man easy and happy in his home. Paul's
story-telling complemented the rhythm of the coffee preparations. His pace harmonised with the gentle cracking of the eggs
into the poacher. Scalding coffee was sipped as the tale unfolded
slowly, like silk slipping from a chair onto the floor.

"When I saw him at the end of last month, he was on top of
the world. I gave him the quarter-ounce deal, top quality black, as
he'd requested. I did wonder why at the time, but paid it no mind.
He'd had it all planned out, you know that, don't you?"

Brown eyes reflected gas flames from the grill, as the dark
blond head leaned towards it to check the toast. "Mmmm. Yes. I
think as soon as the shock passed. The first one that is. We were
not exactly expecting it, especially in such a bizarre manner. I
mean, I knew there must have been a good reason, he never did
anything without a good reason, did he? You've known him a lot
longer than me."

"Yeah, ten years. It seems as if we have always known each
other. Well, on the next visit I took him the quarter bottle of
brandy. I asked him if he had enjoyed the smoke and he looked at
me from under those bushy eyebrows, grinning all over."

" 'Not yet Paul, but I soon will, my dear. I soon will.'

" 'You having a party then, you wicked old thing?' I said.
'Who have you got your eyes on? Not the new young nurse with
the droopy red moustache?'

" 'You'll know soon enough. It was kind of you to bring it up.
I'm not going to offer to pay for it. I've allowed myself the luxury of
spending your money, giving myself a treat.' The old devil just
smirked. 'You never noticed, did you?' he went on. 'I put some
slap on. Just a hint of rouge and a touch of shadow on the lids.'

"I laughed. 'As it happens, you've not lost your touch at all.
It's so well done even I thought you looked remarkably well. I
never gave it a thought that you might be using a bit of slap.'

" 'None of the nurses have twigged. I put it on in the loo,
under that awful neon light. I found it in the old girl's cupboard, the
morning after they took her down to the mortuary. She would
have wanted me to have it. Camp old thing, wasn't she? Her first
old man sold fish in Petticoat Lane before the war.' "

Paul raised his hands to receive the cutlery and side plates,
which he dealt into two settings like an efficient croupier.

"Well, I spent a lovely afternoon up there with him. Looking
back on it, he was bubbling over with life and vitality. I put it down
to his getting over that bout of pleurisy, brought on by the shock

of having to give up his house, to move into an old peoples' Home."

"He should have come to live with us." Brown eyes flickered momentarily from the cake tin to Paul's face. "In fact, I would really have loved it, he would have been no trouble at all. I am a fully qualified SRN. He was a father to both of us. The old wizard brought us together, didn't he?"

"Yes. Like all the important things in his life, he planned our 'casual meeting' with meticulous care, knowing all along we would like each other."

"How many slices?"

"Two. When the Home rang here last Wednesday, to see if he was coming back, or staying with us for the weekend, and did he have enough tablets? I couldn't make any sense of what they were talking about. Then it transpired he'd gone on the missing list. Done a bunk, telling them he was coming to stay with us for a few days. Right in the middle of the winter, an old man vanishes and nobody notices anything wrong for three days. The crafty old fox planned it so well. Even the taxi was hired from a small firm in Paddington, miles away from the Home in Ealing. When the police finally traced the driver, he told them the old man had changed his mind and wanted to be taken to Jack Straw's Castle on the Heath. To meet his son, he said, for a quick whisky, before going on with him to spend the week with the family. The driver never gave it a second thought. He told the police that the old guy was glowing with health. He was well wrapped up in his cashmere coat, woolly scarf and those little fur boots you gave him last Christmas. The driver said he dropped him off at the pub, but refused his offer of a drink and was given a five pound tip. Which is why he remembered him."

"That narrowed the area down, didn't it?"

The brown eyes now came level with Paul's as Don settled himself at the table.

"Worcester sauce?"

"No, just a dash of black pepper. Yes, his timing was perfect, as always. The heavy snowfall that night covered his tracks."

"Him as well as it turned out."

Paul beamed. "Yeah, especially him."

"Actually, I can smile about it now." Don raised his brown eyes from the toast. "That shocking headline in the *Evening Standard*. 'Old man found naked. Frozen to death on Hampstead Heath'."

"The undertaker. Pass me a piece of toast love, please? The undertaker apologised for having to break his legs to fit him into the coffin. The police said there were traces of alcohol in the blood and the autopsy showed traces of cannabis as well."

"That was the brandy and dope you took him up, wasn't it?"

"Yeah. I felt rotten about that, almost as if I had killed him with my bare hands."

Don looked affectionately across at him. "I know, love, you were pretty rough going there for a while. If I hadn't spiked your booze with a couple of Mogadon you would have torn the place apart. Me as well, the way you were performing."

"Ah. So now it all comes out, you are as fucking crafty as he was." Paul set down his knife and fork and laughed delightedly. "Christ, what a pair you two make. No wonder I love you."

Don lowered his eyes coyly to the plate, a triumphant grin spread across his face.

"Yes, well," he mumbled through a mouthful of egg. "You gotta be prepared to take a few risks to keep your lover from going off the rails. I know you'd do the same for me. Better that, than getting roaring drunk and doing damage to yourself. Good job you went out on the bed, though, I'd never have put you in on my own. You are such a big boy."

"Don't you try to get round me, you and them big brown eyes." Paul leaned over the table and planted a kiss and smear of butter on Don's nose.

"More coffee?"

"Mmmm, yes, please. Let's have a slice of cake, love; now, where was I? Oh, yes, that terrible coroner's court and the funeral arrangements, followed by the call from his solicitors. The preliminary reading of the will. No funeral service, just a big dance at Fulham Town Hall in May. After we have got over the shock. He had booked it all up in advance, paid for the hall, the band, the disco and the adverts. All proceeds to go towards this year's Gay Pride Week."

"Pass your cup, love." Don watched as the black liquid poured from the pot. "He thought of everything, didn't he?"

"That brings me round to the call from the solicitor, to go round to see him this afternoon. Everything having settled back into peace and relative tranquillity, so to speak. He didn't have a fortune to leave, a little capital plus the sale of his house. All his papers and photos, spanning the years, to be given to the Gay Archives if they want them. After we've been through them first, of course." Paul then reached into his coat pocket. "That's a special remembrance for you." Leaning over the debris of the tea-table, he handed Don a small box. Don opened it.

"Oh Paul, how lovely! His little diamond ear studs. I'm going to cry. That beautiful, beautiful man." Don's eyes overflowed with tears. Paul got up and came round the table to stand behind him. Bending over, he kissed the back of Don's neck.

"Can I lick the tears off your cheeks?"

Don giggled, cried, giggled and cried some more as Paul's tongue flicked across his face, lapping up the salty tears. They clung together for ages, each silently drawing strength from the closeness of the other.

"Feel better now? Want a big blow?" Paul teased, producing a large hanky from his jeans.

"Oh, shoo. Go away with you," sniffed Don, as he blew loudly into the white cotton square. "I suppose next you'll be telling me that big boys don't cry."

"No, I'd never do that," he said, hugging Don a little tighter.

"What's in that envelope, then?" Don pointed to the lilac oblong next to Paul's dirty plate.

"Yes, the letter. I'd almost forgotten it." He reached over and handed it to Don. "The solicitor wants us both to go up for a formal reading of the full will tomorrow, but this is for the both of us. I've already read it." Don eyed the thin scrawl on the envelope which simply read "Paul and Don". He drew out the letter which again was written in the spidery hand. Don read it. His mouth dropped open. He re-read it, his face a picture of incredulous amazement. He digested and understood the contents. He finally exploded with a whoop as the full meaning of the message sank in. The tears of sadness, a few moments back, were replaced with tears of joy and laughter. He read aloud from the lilac paper:

Au revoir, my sweeties. No fading away for this old queen in a dusty geriatric ward. I've thought about this for many years and planned accordingly. I am pleased you can both share the "transition" with me. Sorry about the need for secrecy though. I hope the dance will be a great success. Till we meet again on another plane of experience. I'll be waiting there to greet you both. Lots and lots of love and happiness ... Francis the First,

Queen of Hypothermia (once removed).
P.S. What a stunning curtain call, my darlings.

JOHN GOWLING
Never Had a Dream Come True

I was at home at nine-thirty on a hot, dark August night when the phone rang. I turned down the variety show on the telly and made to answer it: "Hello, East 7685."

"Is that the emergency service? It's the Crown Vaults here, the gents' toilets are blocked and overflowing" – the old landlord was in quite a flap – "They're having to use the ladies', and the sewage is leaking into the beer cellar. It's urgent, can you send someone straight away?"

"Ok, ok, will do. That's the Crown at Ancoats, on Bremmer Street?"

"Yeah."

"Give us quarter of an hour."

I put down the receiver and unplugged the tv, then went into the kitchen to swill my face – "twenty-six years of bloody acne" – and look in the mirror. As I put on my work jacket and made to leave, I could already smell the musty stink of shit and urine. I locked the mortice and took the lift down to the car pound for the van. Once inside, I took the rubber torch off the front seat and shone it into the back to check our gear hadn't been nicked: the pump, the rods and plungers.

I drove out into the street and, following the yellow lights onto the ring road, made for George's, my brother-in-law's place. I moaned to myself, "He's on call but not on the bloody phone. Just like Dad – keep all the bloody perks on our side of the family, trust nobody. Mind you, who'd trust our Margaret with a van and a phone and my ex-buddy at her disposal? Nobody." As I turned into the dingy terraced street I saw their front-room light on. I pulled over outside the door then got out to knock. I could hear

George inside, rustling with the newspaper, then padding to the door in his stockinged feet. The creamy yellow light of the front parlour spilled onto my face and coarse jacket as he looked down on me. He ruffled his greasy hair and rubbed his eyes.

"Ssh – the little one's just fallen asleep on the settee. 'Sa job?" I nodded. "Sit in the van, I'll be with you in a minute."

"A blocked gents'."

He dropped his eyes and bottom lip, putting his tongue over it: "Ugh – what a way to spend a Saturday night."

He pulled the door to whilst he went back inside, and I sat back down in the van, making out the carbonised job and time sheets prematurely, bent over the steering-wheel, leaning the paper against the metal dash-cowling and writing in wobbly biro. The whole van smelt of rust and rubber and carbon paper and sewage, the smells I'd grown up to.

"Ah, you're wearing Chanel Number Five," George joked as he got in. He had changed into his skinny work vest and jeans and held his windjammer over his knees. "Nearly paid off the mortgage, you know," he went on.

"Eh, and look what you had to do for it. We're fit for nowt else, ended up just like our folks on Lorrimore Street, in bloody bug hutches."

"At least it's my own, John. Why you don't buy a house, I'll be damned. Paying all that rent to the council – that tower block'll never be your own."

"Like so many things," I sighed. I started the van up the rough tarmac street towards the main road. "Well, it never suited me living in a dingy old terraced house like back home. Besides, it's the money. If the old feller went bust, who'd pay my mortgage? At least I'm safe with the council."

"You should have come on the tools, the only way to make money. Not driving the van and doing the books."

I was depressed at how George saw his life as the perfect model; he was a right bloody brother-in-law.

I moved the van out into the middle lane.

"Well, dad said he never wanted me to go down drains."

"Your dad, he spoilt you."

I was shocked. I turned into the fast lane, barely missing an ambulance. "Spoilt me? – More like regimented me. Do you remember when he taught me to box?"

George fell back into his seat laughing. "Eh, and you gave him a black eye."

"Yeah, after that he took to calling me pansy. You know it's all a joke now, but that wasn't how it started. Dad wanted a boy, you know, a real stocky one, not an average guy like me, more like a hobby son, a mate. When I was about seven, before the boxing lessons, he used to come home from work and insist on teaching me wrestling, till he felt my little hard up his backside. A seven year old kid! It was an accident but it shocked him. That kicked the wrestling into touch."

George looked serious and a bit embarrassed; he frowned down, then looked towards me. "You know you were always there right from the start. As a kid, I mean, it came out – you could feel for other guys."

I looked at my watch, then slowed up the van to give us a chance to chat before we got to the job: I knew George had always blamed himself for my missing the boat, and he was always looking for ways to offload the blame. And now I wanted to land a few blows back at him.

"Well, to tell you the truth, George, I did used to blame you a whole lot, I think when you married my fucking sister; but it wasn't that, you'd been put on the straight and narrow by then. Yet I guess it wasn't you. But it *was* you that started it for me. They were only games, George, we didn't know where they'd lead."

With the back of his hand he mopped his brow, as if the sweat had released some feverous tension that now he could talk of.

"That time in Debdale when we were twelve, when we two took Margaret's puppy for a walk and it grew dark as we were talking about sex and coming teenage ..."

I caressed the steering-wheel. "Days of the old schoolyard, George, taking a look at each other in the park. First time either had seen another guy pubic. We was messing with each other for quite a while till the pup heard that cop. And we darted over the park wall with my hands over the dog's muzzle."

George recalled: "Yeah, we came very quick then, and the dog nearly had a nervous breakdown, hahaha ..."

"I used to have fantasies of what if that cop had found us and joined in with us."

"Hahahaha."

"Ok George, it's not that funny."

"Twelve inches of shit on his truncheon."

We turned into the big Oldham Road now, in fits of laughter.

"It was his uniform I was more into, or his boots."

"His helmet." George was bent over double, hissing and wheezing.

"Do you remember – hey George, calm down a bit – when we went on holiday with your mum and dad and you started us wanking in bed, and they said how we'd have to go home if we didn't stop fighting at night?"

"Yeah." George's face solemned. "When we got back to Manchester my folks went round to yours and had a discussion ..."

"Yeah, and my dad says to me something about 'like a pair of little queers.' And my mum said, 'Mrs Evans has had such an embarrassing chat with us and we are quite shocked, but now we know what you've been doing. I don't want you around when George calls for Margaret.' "

He looked ahead as if to stick his head through the windscreen. "Now that really got me, John, 'cos I mean we were only friends. It was only curiosity and then a bit of fun. And you were marked out as the evil influence, and really it was me keep poking that we do it. You could have got married, John. I mean I know they breathed down the necks of me and Margaret till we were down the aisle and with a house, cat and baby. But you could have done it."

"I just knew I was gay, George, didn't I? I think you had brought me out, but you weren't the guy I wanted. I had to get away from home to do it. I have a good time of it nowadays."

We pulled into the pub car park.

"And now for the piss sequence," I announced. I opened up the back of the van whilst George put his wellies on then he stumbled into the pub to find the landlord. I fidgeted with the rods and brought the pump ready for off-loading. George and the ruddy-faced licensee beckoned me into the toilet block. And true enough it was swimming in it. We waded over to the urinal and looked at the drain dome.

"Have you got a cloth or a rag?" I asked the landlord. He handed me a beer towel and I lifted the dome to look down the drain.

"There's nothing blocking it in here, we'll have to try with the manholes and eliminate."

We walked outside. George went over to the council's lid in the drive-in and levered it up.

"It's all clear here and running free."

"Makes it simpler. Least we won't have to get the council out. We can do this tonight. You can leave this to us now. Have two pints of bitter waiting for us in an hour," I winked at the landlord. He ambled back to his glittering little fun house, and as he opened the door laughter spilled out like a stupid musical box.

We paced back in the dark, looking for the pub's junction box.

"Here she is," George shouted. I wrenched it up, and we both stood back from it, quite dizzy. It was full of it.

"Looks like you'll have to go down, George. Let's get the pump out."

It was a two-man job, lifting the pump. Then George kneeled over the hole, dropping the pipe into it, and I span the cord to get the pump chugging. Soon the motor drowned out the juke-box, and sewage gushed out down the yard to the street. We sat on the back of the van and I offered him a Number Ten to smoke away the stench. He struck up: "So here we are together again on another Saturday night. It's not much of a gay life for you, is it?"

"Well, you stop in with Margaret the same, waiting for me to knock with another job. Sometimes in a thunderstorm we're out all night together. Neither of us can think of sex all the time. I mean, how does Margaret cope with 'on call' nowadays?"

"She gets a bit irritated, 'cos she can't plan anything, but at least it means I'm home for part of the weekend nights, instead of down the pub with the lads. I mean, I know she's a bit wary of me being with you. She doesn't look in my underpants or get bitchy over it. It's not as bad as it could be, it's money for the cookie jar. She knows I'm straight. And being brother and sister, I reckon she's got used to you being gay by now."

I thought of my sister, the depressing fool. She certainly got him on the rebound. She went after him like a prize at a fair. I stood up to check how far down the manhole the water had dropped. I poked the tube down deeper into the murk: "Another three feet, another ten minutes."

I went round to the back of the van and George's wellies were outside, he'd pulled the doors closed to change. I went round and sat in the driver's seat and held two more cigarettes in my mouth, to hand him one when he changed. We were still boys in a way, the way he would strip off everything in the back of the van so as not to soil any of his clothes inside the waterproof. When I turned round he was completely naked and kneeling on the balls of his stockinged feet, with his knees apart like a wrestler. I held the two cigarettes against the driving-wheel in my right hand and spoke.

"It's funny how when we were kids we never did it naked, did we? Then how we got separated by being accused of being what we weren't. And now I'm a poof, I always see you naked. It's crazy."

He put his hands between his thighs then cupped his balls and waved his prick at me, rubbing his pubic hair with the meat of his thumb. He laughed. "Still crazy after all these years?"

He looked deep into my face, I looked at his prick and smiled. "It's different now, we've been friends, that's all we ever were. You're straight, and I've got plenty of guys."

His face crumpled (but why? he shocked me); he sat down on his jeans and pushed down the slight erection, then pulled up the legs of the waterproof. "No, I wouldn't now, not with having Margaret and giving you your niece, and you John as family. Your dad did take me as an apprentice. I've often thought I'd like to take it further with you, you're a lot more my scene than Margaret, but it's a shame to complicate it."

He pulled the elastic top up his back to around his shoulders, then squeezed his arms in and zipped and buttoned the front.

"Here, Plastic Man." I lit our cigarettes and handed him one. He sat round and kicked the doors open, replacing his feet in his boots and standing up on the tarmac. After a few long draws he threw the butt and fastened his hood. I shone the torch down the hole so he could see the rungs and the bottom. He put on his gloves and descended into the stink. "Shine the torch," he pointed. "Hand us the torch, I think I can see what's blocking it." He was poking his foot inside the pipe that led towards the council manhole.

"I won't need a rod, it's a thick load of shit, something's collecting it in there. Pass us the crowbar, the bent one, so I can lodge this free."

I passed it down. He held the torch between his knees and clawed into the pipe. "Fucking bastard," he shouted, "I've got it. Here, catch the torch."

He threw the glowing stick up at me, then climbed up, clutching a huge white sack. He blew upwards and spat the dirty water off his face, then sat on the tarmac, his feet still in the hole. He held the ᴜ⸍": in front of his head like an Olympic runner holds a trophy.

"The fucking stupid bastards." He tipped the sack forward and its load of hardened shit fell downward solidly like a five-pound bag of potatoes. It smashed into thick pieces on the tarmac. And above his head he held a giant-sized pair of cotton Y-fronts.

"The bloody drunken louts, anyone flushing their bloody pants down the bog."

I tried to hide my smile from him, but as I hid it the smile became ironic and sinister, so he burst out laughing too.

Inside the van he lay on the grooved floor to unzip the suit, and hold it down whilst he stepped out of it. He was reeking with sweat, the inside of the suit drenched with his musky scent, his body was steaming. I handed him our hospital towel we had requisitioned from another job, then passed him his shorts. Later we loaded the pump and the rest of the tackle back into the van, cleared up the yard, and he smartened himself up. We walked into the pub. "Where's them two pints?" I bawled across the bar. George pulled the landlord inside the bog to sign the 'job done' slip. Then I walked George over to a quiet corner and we sat behind a small table. I rested my elbows: "Another night, another dollar; cheers."

We drank deep, then both of us came up for air at once, our eyes meeting as if we were both about to say the same thing; but there was no thought, just a feeling as if to say "it's me and you". We just quickly shook our heads to snap away the unwordable feeling, then smiled.

"I want to go back," he spoke soft. "If they hadn't closed the door on us. Can I sleep with you, tonight? Look, if we – would you? Just a couple of hours at first. Margaret wouldn't know."

I squeezed his thigh, consoling him as if he had been bereaved. My mind twisted, I felt a shocked frankness on my face: "I don't want to go back. I've gone on to better things. You're my brother-in-law now, my only straight friend who understands and accepts me. It would be like a big hole and my whole family and life thundering down it. I don't want to lose any of you for it. I'm freer with you for not having you. And I don't want to lose you by saying No. That's how I feel George, dead pan."

"Yeah, ok, you respect me, I respect you. But I'm not sorry I asked; and I'm hurt that you don't want me. I want you. I won't stop ..."

"We didn't have the guts, George. They set it up against us and you played right into it." I stood up to leave.

As we drove home I wondered silently over and through the traffic, needing not to speak to him, now worrying over how much longer he would allow me to be his close friend after I had rejected him. And wondering if he'd turn evil on Margaret ... "War, waste and weddings."

I drove him to his door. The upstairs light was now on. Margaret would be reading in bed. "See you, George," I whispered.

"Yeah, take care now John, I mean that." He clutched my hand. "Don't take it so hard ..."

I laughed: "Like the Four Tops said: 'It's all in the game'."

"Yeah ... 1970, our last summer. I've still got that record. We had some times, that record always reminds me of the allotment."

I tapped the steering-wheel and leant over. "Now this is a killer, but I'll tell you I've still got my record too, it always reminds me. Remember 'I never had a dream come true'? Well George, I guess it turned out that neither of us did. I'll see you now. Maybe in a couple of hours if there's a thunderstorm, eh?"

He ran in the house, I drove off thinking of him running upstairs to my sister and coming on all romantic with her, then pretending it was me. And supposing she could read his mind as he was doing it? I thought of the plastic waterproof in the back of the van, the shell of the affection we never explored, of how I might wash it in hot water to revive his scent for me, or even wear it, my naked body inside it, or urinate in it so as to claim him bitterly.

On reaching home I ran straight upstairs with it and threw it blindly in the bath, saturating it in cold water, then hung it up to dry. The shell was now empty. I took a Guinness from the fridge, then took two sleeping tablets to forget, to make tomorrow quite another day. There had always been better guys around than that fool, I'd always known it. Carry on as normal, John.

CHRIS PAYNE
The Sighting

Ted and Sheila had spent a quiet half-hour before nightfall monster-watching. Their Mercedes stood in a clearing by the side of the road pointing towards Loch Ness, a thousand feet deep. They sat in the front seats, Ted dutifully holding the camera ready, while Sheila scanned the view with powerful binoculars. Predictably, there had been little excitement, and Ted, who disbelieved totally in monsters, felt his patience running out. However, they were on holiday, and he was determined to be as good-humoured and tolerant as possible.

"Bloody nuisance how it never shows up while you're on the lookout," he observed, settling down in his seat and pulling his white sun hat over his face. Sheila automatically smiled at the jibe.

"It would be marvellous to see something," she said without losing concentration.

Before every holiday she walked down to the village library and read up about their destination. This thoroughly annoyed Ted, since he didn't like anyone to know more than he did, in case he looked a fool.

This time, amidst the Highland clan history and folklore, the evidence had convinced Sheila that there was a family of strange creatures somewhere down in those opaque waters. She had therefore insisted they spend some time every day watching.

Ted tried to doze off, but he was feeling agitated and annoyed. At work, or motoring to work, he could have angrily taken it out on somebody, but he knew not to risk upsetting Sheila too much on holiday, because of the purgatory he would then endure until she forgave him. So instead he remained agitated and brooded on various events that had fuelled the feeling during the day: an insolent young petrol-pump attendant, traffic hold-ups, a shop that wouldn't accept his cheque card.

"Be careful," warned the disembodied voice of his GP, "No more do's like last year."

He went through the motions of tensing several muscles and then relaxing them, before his mind returned to the maid who had first annoyed him that morning. Her accent grated on him for a start at that time of the day, and he pictured her chatting in it to the old woman who sat alone at the corner table, while he wanted her to serve his bacon and eggs ...

"Be careful," the voice repeated.

"I know," he said aloud, "I'll walk back to that red Mini we saw, and maybe they'll have the route to Invermoran." There was a noted pub at Invermoran, and Ted had left his roadmap on the bedside table.

"They might have gone ages ago," said Sheila.

"Well, I'll flag somebody down then," he grumbled.

"Tell me again how I work this camera, if I see anything," she asked.

"Hold it firm, press *this* switch, and it winds on on its own," he said in words of one syllable.

"Oh, I see. Don't be long."

He couldn't think of a civil reply so he stalked off silently. He hoped she would spot a flotilla of dinosaurs balancing beach-balls, since he was confident she would never work the camera and finish up with no evidence so that nobody would believe her. Unless one bit her, of course. If so, he hoped it wouldn't damage the car.

He stepped into the roadside undergrowth, remembering that the Mini had been well hidden. They had noticed it only because they too were looking for a place to park. Just as he was about to give up, he glimpsed a patch of red in the distance through the leaves.

He picked a route through the foliage and low branches to the secluded spot where the car waited. To his surprise, it contained a man and a woman in an embrace, oblivious to the rest of the world – or surely they would have heard him rustling and crackling towards them. For a few seconds he watched, and decided malevolently to interrupt and embarrass them. Open-mouthed kisses, a hand inside a shirt. But wasn't there something wrong?

Then the young man looked up, sensing a spectator, and Ted realised the embarrassment was entirely his own. He had watched for nearly five seconds, which was far too long. Quite improper. The young man now leant against the car roof.

"Anything I can do for you?" he asked coolly.

"Sorry. I'm parked further along. Wondered if you had a road map?" Ted tried to smile, but his efforts found no response.

"No. We're local."

"Oh," said Ted, brightening. "Then maybe you could tell me the way to Invermoran." It was precisely at this moment that he realised the person still in the car was looking up at him. He too was a young man.

Ted was aware that he was being given directions to Invermoran, but he couldn't concentrate. The man ran through them again. His final words needed some response.

"... So it's only a ten minute drive. Ok?"

"No it isn't ok," Ted growled, pulling himself together. "Messing about with your friend there in broad daylight, and you climb out and behave as if nothing had happened." He saw an opportunity to vent some aggression with no likelihood of retaliation. The maid could complain to the manager; the petrol-pump attendant couldn't care less and showed it; Sheila might cow him with her own aggression; but these two were weak and unprotected.

"It ought to be illegal," he said righteously.

"It is illegal, actually," replied the young man.

"So it bloody well should be, too. I should take your number and phone the police." He intended to.

"And tell them you were spying on us?"

"Spying?"

"That's what they'll think anyway."

"No decent person would want to see your revolting carrying on," Ted laughed. The young man began to make his way around the front of the car.

"I won't be insulted by the likes of you. Or threatened. Now push off."

Ted's throat constricted.

"You're a pair of bloody perverts," he croaked. The car door opened and the other young man stood up.

"We're not interested in your opinions. This is our only chance to meet, so clear off, will you? Go and spy on somebody else."

There seemed no course which would involve less embarrassment, so Ted glared at the two of them, standing side by side as if they were proud of themselves. He turned and made as quick a retreat as he could, amongst the low branches and thorns. A twig almost caught him in the eye.

By the time he reached his own car he still had not regained his composure. Indeed, he was dishevelled as well as shaken. And he always turned purple when he was very upset. As he climbed in silently, breathless and self-conscious, Sheila took her glance momentarily away from the loch. Then she looked at him again in surprise.

"God, what's the matter?"

"I just saw ... " he faltered, unable to say the words.

"You didn't! You did!" She flung herself onto him.

"No, no," he spluttered, as she hugged him.

"Oh Ted, you sweetheart."

"Listen Sheila, I didn't see any monster. You've got it wrong."

She looked hard at him, to make sure he was genuinely flustered.

"Whatever's the matter then?" she asked, holding her face a little back from his.

"Nothing at all."

She paused again, and then said knowingly, "You're kidding. You must have seen something and now you're teasing me. Oh, you know how excited I am about it!"

"Honestly," he moaned, disengaging himself from her. "I saw no monster."

"Well, you saw something," she said expectantly.

"No. Nothing."

"But you said you saw something."

He began to laugh. "Oh God. I merely ran back to the car and made myself breathless. Leave it, can't you?"

"I know. You're ashamed to admit what you saw and prove yourself wrong. Well, I know you too well. You definitely saw something just now."

With this, she knew she'd pushed him as far as she could ...

"Did you ask the route, then?"

"No. I couldn't find the Mini. Let's forget Invermoran and

drive back to the hotel."

Later, as they were preparing for bed, Sheila had another try.

"You did see something," she said with certainty, but softly too, having decided this to be the best approach.

"No I didn't," he replied. "Nothing at all."

And that, he felt, was that. He couldn't ever tell her now, because he'd look a fool, having denied it twice. Even though she knew he had really seen something, she would never know what. He now wished he had told her because it troubled him, and he sat on the edge of the bed, brooding.

He could have walked past either of them in the street, without realising what they were, and he wondered how many more were in circulation. Perhaps one of them was married, and his wife didn't know – which would explain the remark about it being their only chance to see each other. Then, to cap it all, they'd stood and argued with him, unawed by the police, and told him to clear off – Ted usually admired someone with fight in him, but that sort of person wasn't supposed to answer back.

Sheila climbed into bed, rolled over with her back to him, and went to sleep. She would have shared his outrage, he felt sure, if only he'd been able to share the experience that caused it. The clock downstairs struck midnight, and he was still awake, thinking. Thinking about how, at home, Sheila would tell all their friends that he'd seen the Loch Ness monster. However much he denied it, he would be sure to look an idiot. He considered whether it would be easier to agree he'd seen it, but then he would be lucky if someone didn't tell the local paper. All the time those two men, and others like them, would be doing whatever they did, and arguing back.

TOM CLARKSON
Tea at Fortnums

The recurring dream ... tranquillisers, sleeping tablets, homeo-
pathy, hypnotism, and now in sheer desperation, Doctor Bach's
Flower Remedies – but all to no avail. There would be periods of
respite, even as long as two months, when she felt it had finally left
her; but suddenly it was there, flung upon her in the middle of the
night like some dreadful incubus.

The awful cracking sound of the door being forced open like
the breaking of bones, and then the first sight of horror, his feet
dangling in their grubby sneakers: so pathetically vulnerable, the
epitome of his youth, of all the youth in the world, all youth
destroyed.

Oh no, it was unspeakable, she could not bear to think of it;
but most of the time she thought of little else. How many years ago
was it now? Over twenty. Surely you would have thought by this
time the ghost would have been laid?

When she had brought off a good deal, and had thus been
able to divert herself with a little holiday – always a working
holiday of course, for she was continually alert for a bargain to
replenish her stock – then it was not so bad. Exotic scenery,
foreigners who had no connection with her past, a sense of
escape.

But she always came back. Not to the house in Streatham of
course. The specialist had advised her to get a flat. Now she lived
in Shepherd's Market over the shop. It was a good centre for
trade, always plenty of well-heeled tourists staying in the hotels in
nearby Park Lane.

Even so she could not afford to relax. Jack, her late husband, had been very improvident. To work for her living had become a necessity.

Sometimes as a little treat she would take herself to Fortnums for tea. But even there her eyes would dart about shrewdly over the top of a forkful of naughty meringue.

"Please, is this place taken?" A slightly guttural but engagingly mellifluous voice drew her attention.

"No, certainly not."

Mrs Everett removed her bag and gloves from the opposite chair. The lady, who was rather heavily built, squeezed herself in, and that was how she had met Mrs Olsen.

Was she a Swede? She certainly had a throaty sort of voice, something like Greta Garbo's. But there the resemblance ended. Mrs Olsen was obviously a rather common person, expensively over-dressed, her numerous accessories including large diamond rings, which Mrs Everett presumed to be real, and an admixture of rather tawdry costume jewellery. She smelled as if she had bought her perfume from the Pakistani stall in a street market.

But Mrs Everett admired her scarf. It was certainly haute couture. Perhaps a Charvet or a Hermès? A design of scarlet blotches almost like drops of blood, but extraordinarily chic. Mrs Everett quite coveted it. She possessed a white trouser suit, and a "little black dress" which the scarf would have embellished. In the present instance it had been dragged through a vulgar base-metal ring in the form of a monkey's head.

They had begun by talking merely of this and that, as women do when forced into close proximity.

Mrs Olsen admired the cameo brooch Mrs Everett was wearing in her lapel.

"I like nice things," she said, in that purry voice like a cat lapping up cream.

It was an opportunity for Mrs Everett to introduce her business.

"I have a little shop," she remarked, assumedly casual. "Quite near here. I sell bygones, bric-à-brac, that sort of thing. I have one or two quite good pieces of jewellery, if you like that –? One minute, I'm not sure, but I may have a card with me."

She rootled about in her bag as if the collection of cards there secured by an elastic band was non-existent, the one she eventually came up with having come to hand by a happy accident.

"How kind of you. I will most certainly come and visit you before I go back. You are open every day?"

"Every day except Wednesday afternoon, when I take a little time off, like now."

There was a slight hesitation when it came to paying the bill. Mrs Olsen seemed about to make the gesture of collecting Mrs Everett's along with her own, but the latter forestalled her. It was not a good idea to start off by being under an obligation, otherwise Mrs Olsen might expect her to reduce her prices. They agreed to pay for themselves.

Out in Piccadilly Mrs Olsen made profuse exclamations as to how nice it had been to meet, with further promises of visiting the shop at her earliest opportunity; then hailing a taxi was whisked away in a trail of the nasty scent.

It seemed that Mrs Everett had made a good catch. A little judicious handling, and the foreign lady might prove to be, to put it rather vulgarly in the words of the popular song, a "big spender".

A fortnight passed, and Mrs Everett decided that on this occasion her business acumen had failed her.

But no, one afternoon when she had almost written the matter off, the Swiss cowbell over the lintel summoned her from her office in the back premises, and there stood Mrs Olsen.

Today she was wearing a somewhat garish suit of kingfisher blue, with a turban to match, beneath which the tendrils of an obviously bleached coiffure wriggled around her rather fat earlobes, glitteringly endiamonded. There was no scarf for Mrs Everett to covet, but a clip – could it possibly be emerald? – below her visitor's saggy throat evoked a tiny, envious sigh.

"Well, I finally made it," exuded Mrs Olsen. " I've been over to Paris with an American friend" – looking round and poking – "What an attractive little shop!"

Eventually Mrs Everett brought out the velvet tray of rings.

"I like *that*," said Mrs Olsen, removing her glove and picking out a Victorian seal ring, topaz in a setting of brilliants. Her hands were large and rather coarse-looking. She managed to squeeze the ring over the knuckle of her "little" finger, then had some difficulty in getting it off.

She couldn't make up her mind about it. Contenting herself with an Edwardian hat-pin – rather a poor sale from Mrs Everett's point of view, amounting to a mere twenty pounds – she finally took herself off, promising to be back when she had had time to think about the ring.

Two days later she returned, and bought it.

It was the beginning of a relationship, not friendship exactly, but something born out of their individual needs. Mrs Everett required to make money, and Mrs Olsen was apparently lonely. They went to occasional matinées together, art exhibitions, and so on, usually ending up with tea at Fortnums where they had first met. Now business was no longer confined to the shop. Mrs Olsen was invited upstairs, her purchases sealed by a glass of sherry.

Mrs Everett had not suffered the dream for quite a long time, then one night it sprang at her as unexpected as an assassin in the clothes closet.

There were the usual ingredients of shock and horror, but for no known reason, this time Mrs Olsen came into it.

It was she who, when the police cut the body down, leaned over it on the bed. She seemed to have assumed the attitude of the Virgin Mary mourning the Lord after his deposition from the cross.

But that was Mrs Everett's place. She went over to pull Mrs Olsen away – and woke up.

As usual the cold sweat, the terrible shivering. She knew her guilt was the cause. It was her action which had brought about her son's death. He had accused her. She had found the note in her handkerchief drawer, but had disclosed it to no one. She had torn it up into little pieces, and flushed it down the toilet. It had felt like disposing of a foetus.

Yes, guilt; unrelenting, haunting guilt. Yet she had meant well. She had done it all for the best. Johnny was not really gay, she had been convinced of it. She had merely taken him away from a world, a lifestyle, which would eventually have destroyed him. She had not anticipated that he would destroy himself.

She swung out of bed and swallowed a tablet, then another one. Then hobbled into the kitchen to make herself some tea.

By the afternoon, when Mrs Olsen was due to call to look at an enamel patch-box which she had informed her had belonged to Marie Antoinette, she was in control again – a little shaky, a feeling of hollowness, but nothing that showed, she hoped. To boost her morale she dabbed on extra blusher.

Mrs Olsen was enchanted with the little box. It had a view of the Petit Trianon.

Today she was wearing the red-blobbed scarf, and Mrs Everett, over the effusion of the sale, admitted her admiration.

"Then you must have it," said Mrs Olsen.

"Oh no, please – really, I didn't –"

"Please take it," pleaded Mrs Olsen. "You have found so many beautiful things for me – the scarf is a mere nothing."

She unwound it, and flung it about Mrs Everett's shoulders.

"It really does become you," she said. "Much nicer on you than on me."

"Well, if you insist."

"I most certainly do."

"I don't know how to thank you – you are so kind. I'll just go and pop the kettle on."

In the kitchen she preened herself before the small mirror over the sink, a little smile of triumph hovering about her lips. Really, Mrs Olsen was a fool. It seemed propitious that she had bought her victim her favourite chocolate gateaux from the Viennese shop in Soho.

Returning to the sitting-room, the sight that met her eyes nearly caused her to drop the tray. Mrs Olsen stepped forward and retrieved it.

But what had happened?

Mrs Olsen had apparently decided to remove her hat. But not only her hat, her hair also!

The blonde wig rested, curiously congruously, on the table next her gloves and bag from Gucci.

It was no longer a woman thus revealed, but a balding middle-aged man.

"Don't be alarmed," came the guttural voice, whose mellifluous tones were now definitely masculine.

Mrs Everett sank onto the settee.

"Don't you recognise me? But why should you? I must have changed a lot. So have you. We are both considerably older."

"But –?" Mrs Everett could hardly utter.

"I'm Charlie," said the voice. "Charlie Waterhouse. Charlie who was in love with your son."

But this was worse than the dream. Mrs Everett was struck dumb. She moved her mouth, but no sound came out.

Charlie was audaciously pouring out the tea and slicing the cake.

"No sugar," he said, pushing the cup in Mrs Everett's direction, who automatically, like one in a trance, put out a hand and raised it to her lips.

It seemed fantastic to be drinking tea in the circumstances.

Charlie forked into a large wedge of the cake.

"Yummie!" he crumbed out.

"But –" Mrs Everett managed. "But you're dressed as a woman."

"Yes, I'm what's known as a transvestite, dear. I haven't always been one. It happened soon after you took Johnnie away from me. Sometimes I hate myself for it. But it's become a habit. A piece of cake?"

"No – no, thank you," said Mrs Everett in a thread-like voice as if she had turned into a ghost.

"I'm quite well off, you know," continued Charlie. "Could probably buy and sell your little place several times over and not notice it."

"What – what are you doing?"

"You mean now? Enjoying this delicious tea. It's Earl Grey mixed with something else, isn't it? Oh, you mean what do I do for a living. Well, where you sell bijouterie, I sell love."

Mrs Everett looked askance.

"Not real love. Fantasy love. Much more reliable, actually. I run a chain of brothels – male brothels, of course. In Paris, and Rome, and the States, where I live most of the time."

"I don't know what to say," ejaculated Mrs Everett.

"There isn't anything for you to say. What could you say? Johnnie and I were in love, and you destroyed it. It wasn't only your son you killed –"

"Oh, don't, please." Mrs Everett uttered a little, strangled cry. "I didn't mean. I –"

"Oh, yes you did. Why deny it? I repeat, it wasn't only your son you killed. It was me too. After Johnnie's suicide I just lost heart, went to pieces. I was ill for over a year in a mental home."

"No!"

"I'm afraid, yes."

"I – I – can you forgive me? You see, I didn't understand about such things then. It's different today. Times have changed. I –"

"But Johnnie, your Johnnie, my Johnnie, is still dead. Time won't change that."

By now Charlie had joined Mrs Everett on the settee. She shrank away from him, but he edged closer. The sickly scent was stifling.

"The scarf ... " she said. "I must give it back to you."

"No, no, please. It really suits you."

She saw his hands coming nearer. Despite the glittering rings and the pink nail-varnish, they were obviously male hands now: strong, menacing.

"The scarf – it isn't quite right. It needs a slight adjustment – like this."

She could feel his coarse fingers dexterously rearranging the silk, touching her skin.

His face was so close it was bizarre, frightening, a bald head with false eyelashes and rouge and lipstick. And the overpowering scent.

"What a pity," came the voice, no longer mock-feminine, but harsh and rasping. "By rights, you should really die twice, you know."

She saw the terrible smile, as if a snake were smiling, felt the ends of the scarf tightening ...

TENEBRIS LIGHT

Uncle William and Uncle Robert Take Michael Swimming

Uncle William has long, white fingers. Uncle William has a taut, white belly.

"Pass me that towel please, Michael."

Uncle William never calls Michael 'Mick' or 'Mike' or 'Mickey', because Michael is now nine and grown-up.

He smiles and charms, holding out his long white fingers, coyly turned not to show anything very much, which is more of an interesting event than any other. Michael wears shorts with little buttons to protect his little button. Uncle William has satin shorts without any buttons. How he manages to go for a piss has been a worry of Michael's for a long time, perhaps three or four years. There is a glass door to the shower-room which clouds over with steam whenever someone is taking a shower. Except Uncle William, who is a cold-water freak and a soapless-showerer freak and many other sorts of freak, according to Michael's father.

Michael is not sure if he is grown-up enough yet to get into a cold shower which would not make clouds enough to retain his secrets.

After the shower they sit down to eat. Uncle William wears a towel type robe that does not seem to do up very well at the front. Michael is tied up inside his shorts by the buttons down the front and the little bright silver stud clip that holds the top closed.

Knock, knock, who is there?

Uncle Robert has been afflicted with hairy shoulders that make Michael a little uneasy when he looks at him. Uncle Robert is a little fat around the tummy but a dark brown tan hides that a lot. Michael is also a little fat around the tummy, but that is hidden as he is getting good at breathing in when he sits down and at wearing a very baggy tee-shirt after he has had a shower.

The tee-shirt belongs to Uncle William, so is big and strong enough to hide anything.

Michael is not very keen on being kissed by Uncle Robert. Kisses are for lips and shoulders and knees. Not for eyelids that have to be very sharply shut to avoid stabbing of the eye by beard bristles. Uncle Robert is very hairy all over. He kisses Michael on the nose. He kisses William on the lips.

When Uncle William puts his elbows on the table at breakfast, the crease that causes soon fills with the sweat that arrives after a cold shower on a hot morning. The golden hairs, standard in colour and size, act as a guide-line for which direction the rivulet of sweat will take.

Michael thinks it would be jolly to hold his tongue about half an inch below the elbow and half an inch above the table, and catch the drops one by one instead of having orange juice.

Michael does not have orange juice at home.

After breakfast they all three go and sit on the bed in Uncle William's room to wait for him to do his pull-up exercises. Twenty times up, pant. Twenty times down, pant. The muscles on the stomach bulge and then die. Michael pants.

The sun is getting very hot, and all this waiting makes Michael sweat and want to go to the toilet.

William gets up off the carpet and goes to shave at the sink in the bedroom. All the bedrooms in Uncle William's house have wash basins installed in them, which are all the same colour.

Uncle William drops his robe to the floor in preparation for getting finally dressed. Michael does not have too good a view because, at exactly the wrong moment, he is grabbed by Uncle Robert, who throws Michael up and down above the bed, never missing a catch. Uncle William's underpants do not have a space where it is possible to piss through. How does Uncle William manage to piss when he has no slit in his underpants and no buttons on his shorts? Perhaps he puts his hand down inside both of them and grasps his penis strongly enough to pull it up and over the elasticated top. Perhaps he has to take his shorts and underpants right off and then stand above the toilet. Michael is glad that he has clothes which he can wear while pissing.

In his shorts in the car, Michael's legs are starting to stick to the seat. He sits held firmly between Uncle Robert's hairy legs, which spread open as wide as they can go to allow enough room for Michael to sit in the front seat of the car, where they can all look out of the same windows and see the same vista.

Michael fits well into the shape of Uncle Robert's slightly fat bit, the fat acts as a hot pillow. With one hand on each hairy knee, Michael is able to raise himself when his legs stick too much and rearrange his position with Uncle Robert. When the car turns a corner a bit too fast, Michael can twist in surprise and place his left hand firmly onto Uncle Robert's penis. Michael would really like to know if Uncle Robert has a hairy penis and is trying hard to find out by imagining the car to be turning too fast at every corner.

Uncle Robert is getting rather hot in the sun.

Michael sits on his hands by the swimming pool. He does not like the water very much. The uncles are diving in and getting out and diving in and swimming and then getting out to dive in again. Michael does not have a swimming suit as he does not like to swim so he wears his white underpants to sit in the sun. Both of the uncles have red swimming suits which have no slits to piss through. Perhaps they piss in the water. Michael giggles.

The changing room for men is an area of wooden slatted screen which has three sides and a big picture in silhouette of a man wearing swimming trunks with a square cut to the holes where the legs go through, so there is enough room for him to piss out that way without having to remove the trunks.

As Uncle Robert gets out of the pool, the water running off him makes all the hairs on his body lie flat and close to him. The hairs on his body do not stick up in any place except for a tuft at the centre of his swimming suit where his two legs meet. Michael feels quite sure now that Uncle Robert does indeed have a hairy penis and that is where these rogue hairs are sticking out from. The sun is getting hotter still, so Michael goes and puts his toes in the water. The uncles jump in and splash him deliberately, which annoys Michael. While he is wiping the water out of his eyes, one uncle, he is not sure which, grabs each of his legs with a hand, stretches them apart and pulls Michael onto his shoulders.

Michael reaches out and grabs the uncle's hair to make sure he does not drown. It must be Uncle William, as the hair is slightly oily with hair cream. As he swims across the pool with Michael on his back, a tiny trail of grease lights the water in the same way as a snail's trail lights the earth.

The water is such a cooling after the heat of the sun and Michael is not scared of the water when he is on Uncle William's back. He starts to giggle and slowly, feeling wicked, allows a tiny stream of piss to emerge from his penis.

It is bright yellow-green in colour and makes a trail all the way down William's back, but is soon washed away with the force of the swimming to join the snail's trail.

William is not aware of what has happened, but continues to swim.

Robert, swimming alongside, does notice and as his eyes meet with Michael's, he grins a wide, tanned grin and pisses into the water with a total disregard for the other swimmers.

DAVID REES
Aiming High

Five of us from Exeter on a night out in Bournemouth: Phil, Martin, Andy, Neil, and me. Phil's lover Brian was working that Saturday, so Phil was hoping for a bit of macho on the side. He never told Brian – who was anything but macho – about these escapades. Martin wanted chicken. His other half Graham was quite well aware of what would happen and he didn't mind: they never had sex together these days. Andy and Neil were lovers. Andy was my ex-affair; he didn't leave me for Neil, but Neil was the eventual replacement. They were not sharing a bed that night; Andy was going to a birthday party and staying with Ian and Tom, while Neil was to sleep in the spare room at Jim and Tony's. The reasons for this temporary separation were somewhat obscure, but I didn't like to probe; it was none of my business. I felt sorry for Neil. He was obviously in love with Andy, whereas Andy, I thought, was no more than flattered by the attention.

I was the only one completely unattached. Except for my brief fling with Andy, I'd been alone since Kevin left me last year. I'd not found Mr Right in those long, rather boring twelve months, nor even Mr Compromise. I'd met several Mr Bed-and-Breakfasts, and I didn't imagine an evening at the Apollo Club would give me anything more than the usual one-night stand, if that. However, it couldn't be worse than my last adventure in Bournemouth, when I'd ended up with a mad, drunk ballet dancer who'd insisted on performing Swan Lake at two o'clock in the morning (the record player on at ninety ear-splitting decibels). When we eventually got down to it, he provided for a lubricant half a pound of Anchor butter.

Most of the conversation in the car on the way up to

Bournemouth was the usual talk about sex: a predictable, repetitive circle from which there seems to be no exit. Big cocks, medium cocks, small cocks, what X or Y were like in bed, then – once more – big cocks, medium cocks, small cocks.

"Why the fascination?" I asked Phil.

"I'm not *really* fascinated," he said. "But a big one helps; you must admit that, Jack. And I do like a man to have a moustache."

"Why?"

"So that he looks like a man."

I think moustaches unattractive, but ... well ... a *very* small penis is a disappointment. Phil and the others, of course, were discussing contact that was sexual and nothing else – trade; in their lovers they presumably found something more complex and more interesting than hairy upper lips and inches of erectile tissue. Like emotions perhaps, or compatibility. I certainly had. And I wasn't obsessed with trade: I hated one-night stands. Though I hated even more the idea of not finding anyone, of sleeping with no one beside me. Particularly if the others all scored; that would emphasise my loneliness, push me further down the slippery slope of self-pity. So I too spun, willingly and unwillingly, in this circle with no exit.

"It's fabulous to have a night off!" Phil said. "Brian's so clinging; he just can't leave me alone for a moment! But he never tricks. Doesn't want to. I can't understand why." Then he added, as an afterthought, "I expect I'll appreciate him all the more when we go home. I always do."

Interesting, I thought, that he looks like the kind of man he lusts after – short hair and moustache. So many of us, Phil included, try to turn ourselves into a replica of the man of our dreams. I've always fancied men with big arm muscles. My biceps are one of the bonuses of weight training: I look at them in the mirror and say, Jack, you look good. Sexy. So: the more your ideal lover eludes you, the more likely you are to imitate his looks, his hair-style, his clothes. Compensation.

"Look at *that*!" Martin said, once every ten minutes. "Just get an eyeful of *that*!" "That" was any youth we drove past; it did not matter if he was ugly or attractive, tall or short, fat or thin: if he was nineteen or under, Martin's attention was riveted. "Did you see *that* one?" He was like a kid let out of school.

Andy, who was driving, contributed little to the conversation. Neil and I talked for a while about gardening, and mutual friends and acquaintances. I looked out of the window. The road from Exeter to Bournemouth is beautiful, but in the gathering

November dusk there was little to see. Occasional chestnuts and
beeches in autumn flame; a light out in the Channel; the shapes of
hills. I pictured in my mind's eye the villages in summer, their
thatched, sandstone cottages with garden flowers bright as a
child's painting; the steep streets of Lyme; the enormous curve of
England from the heights between Bridport and Winterborne
Abbas – chalk, green downland, the long arc of pebbles out to
Portland, and the reminders of a very ancient past: a landscape in
which antiquity is still so strong in its hold that it would not be
surprising to see a man dressed in animal pelts and wielding a club
emerge from behind the ramparts of a prehistoric fort.

Neil was deposited at his friends' house, and Andy went off
with Phil to Ian's birthday party. (Phil had been promised a sofa
there for the night, if no other arrangement occurred at the
Apollo.) The club does bed and breakfast, and I'd booked a room;
the owner Steve is an old friend of mine. Martin had decided,
characteristically, on an expensive gay hotel. His room was full of
intercoms and dimmer switches that put him into a good mood at
once. He loves to surround himself with electronic gadgets:
they're status symbols; they allow him to think he's arrived. We
mucked about with these for half an hour and giggled a lot. He has
the effect of making *me* feel like a kid let out of school.

I'm not being fair to him. I've never heard him make a bitchy
remark about anyone, and he's one of the kindest, most
hospitable people I know. I like his eyes: very dark and warm, all
the more noticeable because his hair and his beard are almost
blond. People take advantage of him, calling round on the
pretence of needing to see him, whereas all they want is to drink
his booze. On his own, he's much nicer than when he's in a crowd;
his conversation then isn't confined to cock sizes and chicken-
ettes.

After we'd finished playing with the gadgets, we washed and
shaved, and debated what to wear for the club – all five of us, true
queens as we are, had brought far more clothes than were
necessary for one night away from home. We made up our minds,
then changed our minds, put on what we'd originally thought of,
splashed Lagerfeld on our faces, and went out for a meal.

At an expensive restaurant. Well, why not once in a while?
An excellent meal, excellent wine, and Martin was excellent
company. We had a long conversation about whether we should
buy a pub that was being sold off dirt cheap by the local brewery.
And turn it into a proper gay meeting-place: we don't have such a

thing, just one bar of a straight pub where we're barely tolerated, though the landlord is more than greedy for our pound notes. Neither Martin nor I had any real intention of putting our money into a pub, but it was fun to play along with the idea. By the end of the meal we'd convinced ourselves that it was a marvellous proposition: we'd even got as far as the details of what food we'd serve – Graham would cook it – and how much we'd charge for a bottle of Pils and who we could trust in the gay community – Andy – to take over the business when we wanted a night off. I said I would ban Kevin for life the moment he set foot in the place, which Martin thought highly amusing.

We arrived at the Apollo in a very good mood. Andy and Phil were already there, but Neil was missing.

"Oh, he's staying indoors," Andy said. "His friends don't like this club."

"Where are *your* friends?" I asked.

"Ian and Tom? They're at home ... they don't like it here, either." He laughed. "But I wasn't going to let that stop *me* from coming!"

I wondered if it would be worth any of us, in any sense, coming: the Apollo, for a Saturday night, was far from busy. Gay clubs, as *the* scene to go to, have a short life-span. The Apollo was four years old, and therefore regarded as an ancient, tatty artiste whose mascara had long since become smeared. In fact it's a very pleasant place. The local crowd had shifted their allegiance to Southampton, which, they claimed, had the best disco between Land's End and Dover. One disgruntled customer whom Steve had expelled had got his revenge by chartering a fleet of coaches which swished the Bournemouth queens off to Southampton every Friday and Saturday. Steve was philosophical about this. "In a couple of months they'll all be back here," he said. "Still ... I hope the buggers turn into pumpkins at midnight!" I liked Steve: round, firm face and friendly green eyes. I had admired him in many different situations – the death of his lover, hassle from the police about licences, a show that had flopped. Steve was one of the survivors: he had sang froid, a gift for being undramatic.

Andy had brought us up; Neil was to drive us back. I was in charge overnight; Phil's turn was tomorrow afternoon. Martin, whose car it was, couldn't drive: the breathalyser crystals had all gone green, or whatever they're supposed to do. So, I thought, I have problems. If everyone scores and vanishes to distant parts of the New Forest or the Isle of Purbeck, how shall I round them all up in the morning? I decided I wouldn't let any of them leave without giving me a telephone number.

If indeed any of us wanted to rush off into the depths of Hampshire and Dorset. The prospects didn't look good. We spent a long time drinking with each other, then dancing together – Andy and I very serious and silent, really into the music, Phil and Martin messing around; then Phil and I just shuffled because we were talking, while Martin and Andy did some crazy last tango to out-tango all last tangos; then Phil and Andy all serious once more (it was Donna Summer) while Martin and I indulged in a grotesque and faintly obscene wriggle.

After that it all suddenly happened. Martin was dancing with a mock chickenette (he had a moustache and was a bit thin about the temples, but to Martin he passed for nineteen, perhaps, in the dim, flattering light). Andy was being kissed by a butch, dark-haired man with a moustache. The blond and the dark: Andy's greatest asset is his fair hair – curly, long, almost to his shoulders: Phil was with an extremely attractive blue-eyed Viking type. And I was having a drink bought for me by a tall, muscley guy with a perm, not bad-looking, rather like a second division centre forward. He was very camp, however, limp wrists and so on. But I thought, things are so often the opposite of what they seem; it probably meant he would *not* turn over in bed. I too give out confusing signals, I suppose. I'm always told that I seem so butch, so masculine, that I *must* want to screw.

"What is Andy up to?" I asked Phil.

"Tricking on Neil, I guess."

"Poor old Neil!"

"Ah ... he'll never know. What does it matter? You're only young once."

"Do you think I need a phone number?"

"No. That guy is staying here, at the Apollo."

"And Martin?"

"He's taking that one to his hotel."

"And you?"

"I can't be bothered. I've had a nice evening ... a good drink, some fun dancing ... I don't want to go to bed with anybody just for the sake of it."

"Your Viking's pretty good-looking."

"Not good enough! To tell you the truth – and I'd only admit it to you, Jack – I'd prefer to sleep with Brian."

Phil perhaps was more faithful than I had thought. All that talk ... just fantasy. The fact that Brian didn't mind his lover going off to a club without him, didn't mind him staying out for the night, probably meant that Phil was less inclined to sleep around than if he was tied up in the straightjacket of jealousy and possessiveness. If only Kevin had been like that! I might have held on to my respect for him. Phil and Brian, I began to think, must have rather a good relationship.

Martin left with his balding chicken; Andy and the dark-haired man disappeared upstairs. The one I was with, Paul, turned out to be an employee of the club; "the breakfast lady," he said.

"So we don't have far to travel, then?"

He laughed. "Just two flights of stairs. No need to ring for a taxi."

I was right in my guess. On our own, in the privacy of his bedroom, the camp manner stopped at once. Pillow talk was simply two gay men: intimate, natural, male. I liked his nakedness, and his fingers very gently touching the hairs on my thighs, caressing the skin just below my hips, and his mouth on my cock which was eager now and impatient: I liked the long time before he pushed my legs back, the slow, considerate way he entered, the unrestrained vigour that followed. The sweat of his skin, his harsh breathing as his sperm throbbed in me. And too, the expression in his eyes (I'd been a good fuck, I knew that; I could tell), the long time he stayed in me, the flexing of his cock inside like a whispered word. The smile on his face. Then sucking me, and very quickly I came, arms stretched out like arms in a painting of the Crucifixion; then the smile that told me he knew I'd found him as good as he had found me. Lying in his arms, kissing. His right hand, turning off the bed-side light. Falling asleep, curled round each other.

At breakfast, he camped it up like mad, waving toast-racks and teapots all round the room and generally getting himself sent up by all the guests. They called him Brenda. He flounced back and forth, mincing in knee-high leather boots (on tiny, almost stiletto heels), replying to the banter like someone who'd learned his lines in this particular scenario years back. I sat alone, in tight jeans and a tee-shirt which showed off my chest and arm muscles to their best advantage: and laughed to myself as I thought of the difference between us, and the difference – which no one would realise – in bed. I could feel him, inside me.

Three young men – from the Midlands, to judge by their accents – were sitting at the table next to mine. Their conversation was mainly about Chris, a friend of theirs, who was apparently still in bed. How, they wondered, had he got on last night? The guy he went off with was extremely cute. The number of men Chris had had this week! Incredible! Yes, very cute; curly-haired blonds were always attractive.

It dawned on me: this was the person Andy had slept with. At that moment, Chris himself arrived and was greeted with a barrage of laughter and questions. Where is he? What was he like? What time did you get to sleep? Was he a big boy? Are you seeing him again?

Chris said nothing, just giggled as if he was very embarrassed, and helped himself to cornflakes. Come on, Chris; what's the matter? You aren't normally as quiet as this! Tell us, what was it like? Good?

More giggles.

"You're referring to my ex-lover," I said. I've never, in my life, produced a silence so sudden and so profound. To see people staring with open mouths is, in reality, not a common experience, even if in a bad novel it can happen on every other page; but here was the phenomenon, in front of my eyes for the first time.

"I know!" said Chris. "I know! That's why ... "

I laughed. "I really don't mind what you say! It won't bother me in the least." I raised my arms, put my hands behind my head, and leaned back in my chair. I like doing that: it makes me look relaxed, and at the same time it shows off the biceps impressively. Even threateningly. "Where is Andy, if it's not a rude question? It's my job this morning to round them up, the other four."

"He didn't stay all night," Chris said. "He went back to his friends' house, the ones who gave the birthday party. That other guy waited for him, the one with the suntan and the moustache."

"Phil."

"Yes."

"But ... how did they get to Ian and Tom's? I had the car."

"They took a taxi."

"Oh."

All four Midlanders stared, for a long moment, in silence. I stared back. Then they began to talk among themselves; what time should they leave if they wanted to be in Birmingham at five o'clock that afternoon? When they got up to go, Chris grinned and winked at me.

Paul, still doing his Brenda act, flapped across the room and cleared the table. "Out-rage-ous queens, those four," he said. "You can't im-ag-ine, Jack, what I've had to put up with, all week!" Then the mask dropped, so completely I was quite startled. In his ordinary voice he said, "Are you returning to Exeter today?"

"Yes. Not till this afternoon, though."

"Ah." He smiled a little sadly, and touched my arm. "Well in that case," he said, "I daresay I'll see you next time you come to Bournemouth. You *will* come again, I suppose?"

"Of course. Steve's an old friend. I'll be here ... oh ... soon after Christmas."

I went round to Ian and Tom's, drank coffee, and took Andy and Phil away. Then prised Martin out of his hotel: he was reluctant to leave as he'd taken a fancy to the boy who worked in the kitchen. I passed the steering-wheel over to Phil, my job finished. He drove us slowly through the middle of town, where we bought Sunday papers, then up on to the cliffs; we parked in the Boscombe Overcliff Drive. Neil, apparently, was not to be collected till later in the afternoon; the friends with whom he'd stayed were giving him lunch. Would Andy, I wondered, tell Neil about Chris? I guessed not. He seemed determined to keep things as casual as possible; if Neil found out and was annoyed, Andy might even be glad: he would have an opportunity, if he wanted one, to break it off. It wasn't, I thought, the kind of relationship in which one of the pair, bored with screwing his partner, tricked, then returned, now really wanting to make love.

I looked at the sea, and remembered other times I'd been here. Maybe happier times: with Kevin, staying the night, the two of us, at the Apollo. Was I ever happy with him? I liked the stability, being the "other half"; oh yes, and all the certainties and the shared home and the companionship and the sex (when it was good, which it wasn't always) and the occasional, very occasional, aura of magic about him. But happier than now? Yes ... a lot happier than now.

The sea was rough. Blue, except where the sun dazzled its surface to pewter or glittering gold. White foam pushed up the sand. I love the great sweep from Swanage round to Hengistbury Head, and the Needles: sharp nails on the Isle of Wight's foot. Old ladies walking their dogs. On the other side of the road the solid houses of the nineteen-twenties, symbols of security. If I were a house I'd elect to be one of those Japanese paper creations, designed to fall down with a minimum of fuss in the first earthquake. There'd be less shock, less destruction.

We returned to the club: two o'clock on Sunday was the hour of the cabaret. Bizarre some of these little shows could be; Herr Issyvoo's Berlin would have liked them. "But today you're in for a disappointment," Steve said. "It's a local lad, without any real experience. He begged us and begged us to give him a spot so we eventually did, just to shut him up. I bet there'll be more people in today than usual; all those dizzy queens who fucked off to Southampton last night. They'll come in just to take the piss out of him."

"Are you suffering from the competition?" I asked.

"No. Not really. A bit down on this month last year, but that's the recession. It's a quiet time – in summer we're rushed off our feet, but winter's one long yawn."

"Kevin been here recently?"

"In September, for just one night. With somebody, I think." He paused. "Do you ever see him now?"

"No."

Steve shook his head. "All those years. After all you did! Bloody shame!"

"Maybe."

We smiled at each other. A lot of sympathy. "Strange the effect the recession has on clubs. During the week we have a few in. Not many, but always some. Easy to guess who works; at midnight, half-past twelve, they drift off home. That leaves a hard core who stay till we close at two: the unemployed. And that happens *every* night of the week."

"I'm surprised they can afford it."

"So am I! Amazed, in fact! To be quite honest, this place is only keeping alive during the week on the money we get from them. Dole money! Mad, isn't it! Things are never what they seem."

"Very true. Brenda, for instance."

Steve laughed. "You should know, dear." He looked at his watch. "We'd better go downstairs. I just hope La Lola's cabaret isn't going to be one almighty fuck-up."

It wasn't. Nor was it the best I'd ever seen: La Lola was a clever conjurer, and some of the drag was ok. His appearance as a nun, smoking a cigarette in a holder shaped like a crucifix, amused me. The queens who watched were almost polite.

We said our farewells to various people, then we drove home, picking up Neil en route. At Poole we stopped for Phil and Martin to phone their lovers.

"I shall have an evening in front of the fire," Phil said, when he returned to the car. "The tv on. Brian and I will catch up on the gossip. Early to bed, and make love. Great!"

"The same, I think, for me and Andy," said Neil.

"Get him to tell you about last night," Phil teased. "He went to bed with a *gorgeous* man! *Huge* cock! *HUGE!!*"

"Better not have done."

Andy poked Phil in the ribs, and they both grinned. Neil's innocence was almost pitiable. But unrequited love was always pitiable and somewhat absurd, particularly if you didn't realise that it was unrequited.

I left the others in Exeter and went back home. No further down the slippery slope of self-pity than I was before we set out on Saturday afternoon: but no further up it, either. He is no better, he is much the same. I'd had a pleasant week-end. I'd gone to Bournemouth with two ideas in mind – to get screwed, and to enjoy myself in the company of old and trusted friends. I'd achieved exactly that, no more, no less. Are my aims too low? Why am I so *sad*? Because, Kevin ... the house is fallen that none can build again.

I can't finish it like that. The following Thursday I met Tim: attractive, taller than me, blue-eyed, long blond hair, Scorpio, easy to talk to, interesting, intelligent: yes, I know it sounds just like a *Gay News* advert. We went to Bristol for the weekend, to the Unicorn Club – a very good disco – and danced our tits off. We arrived home at God knows what hour and had utterly superb sex. Scorpio and Taurus, I read only yesterday, are the best possible combination in the entire zodiac for sexual pleasure. As far as a relationship is concerned, it never starts at all or it endures for life.

Tim, as I write the ending of this story in Harry's flat in London, I wonder what you are doing: I hope you've imposed some order on the chaos you tell me is your life, for I remember you thought this two-day absence would help you to work things out, come to conclusions, make decisions, all those old clichés that are shorthand for vast seismological changes.

It didn't work. The Scorpio and Taurus that never get started.

But I can build that house again. Again and again and again, if necessary, for all the rest of my life, I suppose. You can't aim higher than that. I suppose.

PETER ROBINS
The Lavender Tortoise

It's a town much like any other that's been spawned by a harbour. Most of the small craft in the basin are owned now by weekenders but we've still a crew or two putting out to deeper waters for lobsters – their principal customers being restaurants around the bay. Nor would anyone recommend this bar as anything special. I've drunk in a dozen like it myself around the globe. Might well be why I chose it, with a view of the fairway and a shelf behind me colourful with bottles I've sampled more than once in Rio, Sydney and Cape Town. Not that I'd call my clientele cosmopolitan. A fair few are locals who totter in, plonk themselves on a stool by the door to commiserate about the bed-and-breakfast trade, then wander off into the evening.

Furthest from the door, on the near side of the space invaders machine, is the corner where my gay customers cluster. Ten years on some details blur a little, but I'm certain I didn't inherit any of them from my predecessors. It was after I'd tarted the place up – the odd yard of fishnet over the window and a dozen glass balls hung around the walls – that they began to make the bar a weekend habit. Quite early on I began to expect that Sandra would sail in around eight on a Friday evening and Lennie would join her at near on ten.

After fifteen years in the Merch you can't fool me easily when it comes to human nature. Long before closing time that first evening I saw her, I knew Sandra wasn't after me or Lennie any more than he fancied her. I wasn't so certain from the start that he hadn't taken a shine to me. That didn't repel me. I'd bunked up with gays, even drag artistes, at the end of many a leave. And if I'd let them have a bit, where was the harm? Very kind and thoughtful people they can be. Anyway, to have Lennie giving me a sheepish come-on cheered me no end (not that I showed it) whilst I was working up the business. It's always nice to be needed, especially if you're putting it on a bit amidships as I was, being thirty-five.

Their behaviour in the bar was exemplary, I'll say that. Some contrast with the old half-Nelson routine I often had to dish out to the visiting bourgeoisie on a Saturday night when they'd taken a few on board. Sandra and Lennie, on the other hand, soon became friends – still are – and, as might be expected, they were joined soon enough by Frank and Tony. Who met who, where and in what circumstances I never enquired, knowing, as many of us do, how the world spins on a warm April night by the harbour walls from Bergen to Brisbane.

Many's the pleasant evening my unlikely quartet passed at the quieter end of the bar. No trouble at all. What with television documentaries and bedroom topics being aired more openly in the papers, family groups who kept to the promenade door end accepted them too. The last sniggers stopped pretty sharpish after I'd reminded one gaggle of yobbos that silver from one end of the bar was as good as it was from the other.

Soon enough I was being invited with the others to Lennie's place over a disused warehouse in a quiet cul-de-sac. Very homely he'd made it too, inside and out. The old yard had been tidied and was sprouting everything from cabbage roses to smashing little green-topped tomatoes. Not that he could take all the credit. An endless supply of fresh fish as fertiliser had to be part of the answer.

One Saturday late in spring it was that Chick burst on us like the advance guard from another planet. The old days of sports jackets and club ties are over long since and we accept jeans and sweatshirts as commonplace, but Chick had a style all his own – or so it seemed to us in the backwaters. Take his hair. Whatever colour his parents blessed him with, it wasn't lavender. A lavender punk, would you believe? Just as well the lighting at the sharp end of the bar was subtle. Even so, that lacquered fan of lavender wafted under the lamps like fronds of pampas grass in the Mombasa Harbour breeze. He'd badges from the collar of his rainbow shirt to the six turned up inches of his orange denims. A walking catalogue of good causes he was. And his glasses. In these days of contact lenses, no one convinces me he needed sequinned flyaway specs with lenses that wouldn't have disgraced a national observatory.

That very first night I honestly supposed he'd just hitched into town with his three bulging backpacks. Lennie assured me they'd all spotted him around for a week. He unloaded those packs in the corner and, when drinking-up time came, began hoisting them on again methodically, one on either shoulder and the third across his back. One or other of the buckles was sure to burst under the strain and so, with a regularity we could all predict, pamphlets, unmended socks, paperbacks and more badges would cascade over my tartan carpet like an auto-biography. Knowing this would happen, the others would make their way to the door, leaving Chick to repack and then struggle after them, bowed to forty-five degrees and slowed by his paraphernalia.

"Like a tortoise," I couldn't help smiling into the glasses as I rinsed them, "a bloody lavender tortoise."

It wasn't long before I'd sussed that Chick had a soft spot for Lennie. I couldn't have sworn that Lennie just wasn't having any. People can be secretive. Certainly he didn't appear aware of the symptoms. If there was any lusty sparkle in those grey eyes, it was for me. There was a sadness about Chick's devotion. Extra eager to stand a round he was when Lennie's glass was still a quarter full, though we all knew you only draw peanuts for tearing tickets at the end of the pier. Discovering that we usually foregathered at Lennie's after hours on Saturdays, Chick made Sunday after-noons his own and expected us there for tea and biscuits.

No more than a month, if that, after Chick erupted on us, he caused me a right load of mental anguish. By then, of course, we no longer made cracks about him leaving town any moment, because he went nowhere without the backpacks. Did he even remove them when he managed to score, I wondered? Not that there was any flood of evidence that he'd done so since we'd met him.

That particular evening, I noticed him unbuckling one of the damn things while I was at the blunt end of the bar serving a couple of Hooray Henries, with their stockbroker's fingernails and made-to-measure blazers. If I thought anything, I'd say it was that Chick was about to underline a point he'd been making by reference to his portable library. Not a bit of it. When I ambled back with his usual cider there was a darn great wad of something called GALES – some gay and lesbian news-sheet – spread across my bar.

"What's all this then, Chick? Got your own John Bull printing outfit in there too, have you?"

He peered at me like I was shrivelling to nothing.

"Want to ask a favour. Would you be prepared to sell these once a month at the corner of the bar?"

"Don't know about that, Chick. Hold fast while I get Lennie another shandy."

The answer had to be No , but I didn't want to upset him, either as customer or friend. Certainly I didn't want mutterings of homophobic behaviour that he was always on about around the town levelled at me, because they wouldn't have been true. I set Lennie's drink down and spoke very reasonably and quietly.

"See it my way, Chick. I run a seaside bar. Do I sell _Angling Times_? I do not. Do I push the local parish mag? Not at all. I sell beer. Newsagents sell periodicals. Have a cider on the house to show no ill feelings."

Chick shook his head sternly.

"You know none of the newsagents would take it."

I shrugged and he fell back to what I guessed was his baseline.

"Can I flog it round the bar each month then?"

I just stood there, wondering if any of the others would join in and if so who they might back. Lennie sided with me, as I might have foreseen. I was glad, because I knew Chick would listen to him, even if he swore it was raining pickled choirboys.

"But who'd buy it, Chick? We're all there is. Don't want you getting a knuckle sandwich in your mouth trying to preach to the unconvertible, do we?"

To console him, we all bought a copy and he stuffed the rest back into his pack. For some weeks after he was unusually withdrawn. I felt his mind was elsewhere. Brooding, maybe, on his unrequited love for Lennie or – and I for one hoped not – planning to leave us for more promising missionary fields. I didn't ask, nor did the others, though I'm certain they noticed the change in Chick. So there was this dampener on our get-togethers until we were at his place one wet Sunday afternoon about six weeks later. He perked up there, being on his home ground, and had been advising Sandra to stand up more firmly for her rights. She'd read (or said she had) the clutch of pamphlets he'd lent her and no doubt he felt she was ready for more than theoretical support for her lesbianism.

"You don't really suppose I haven't tried to make contact all these years, Chick?"

The resignation in her tone brought Chick to his feet before she'd coughed, stubbed her cigarette and added, "Got any suggestions for coping with the aged parent so that I can get away for more than a couple of hours?"

"We shall bring people to you."

"Oh, very good. I like it. So what do I do – shiver starkers on the shingle while you snap me as Venus rising once more from the waves and panting for it?"

Chick faced her sternly and wagged his right hand in her face.

"That's self-oppressive. I have a plan Sandra, so you'd just better trust me."

It was drizzling heavily by then. No one had bought a new disc that week and the video of a Bette Davis oldie hadn't materialised so, what the hell, we all listened. Realising that he had an interested audience, Chick stood, back to the window, hands on hips, to make his announcement:

"I intend to open a gay club."

Initially there was a resonating silence and then Sandra began to laugh almost hysterically.

"Chick, old darling, the very last train comes back from the smoke at nine-fifteen – earlier on Sundays – so count me out for starters."

"Here," Chick countered as a decisive postscript.

Frank choked on his cup of Earl Grey and Tony sat gawping. They'd lived – or maybe I mean existed – in their semi-detached next to a police sergeant and his wife for twelve years, never entertaining guests and so certain that no one in the whole world suspected they might be lovers. Frank, one might say, was a bit naive but didn't lack humour.

"Chick," he suggested, "you should have a late-night series of your own. A gay club here has to be the joke of the season."

"I was never more serious. I've made enquiries. It's a dream I've had for years."

There was a fractional pause and I thought a slight pensiveness as he went on,

"Tried it once somewhere else, but this time it's going to happen. Now, Lennie, if I could move to your place we could base the club there."

Crisis time, I thought. What a time and place for a proposal. Was Lennie still unaware of Chick's interest in him? I waited for the snigger from Frank and Tony, but it didn't happen. Their thoughts seemed elsewhere as they considered the project. Sandra too was genuinely interested in the scheme. I hadn't the heart to take Lennie aside and caution him. It could have been construed that I was grinding a personal axe: a) through being keen on Lennie though not prepared to admit it, and b) losing trade from the bar to a rival club. Not that even a successful venture would be sufficient to endanger my overdraft.

"Must admit that running a candy-floss stall doesn't play havoc with my energies," I was amazed to hear Lennie saying. "Could we really make a go of it, Chick? Don't see why we couldn't operate from here."

"Haven't got the scope. Too little space here for the garden bar."

It wasn't only my own eyebrows that were beginning to float. Chick returned to the more tender part of the subject.

"Ok then, if I bring my gear across this week then, Lennie?"

"Well, I suppose so. There's the spare bedroom ..."

I caught Frank nudging Tony as they sat in their slightly mousey way side by side on the divan. The implication of both question and response wasn't lost on Sandra either.

"I like the idea of the garden bar. 'Tisn't as if we're in the north of Scotland."

"Let's hope it's better than this for the launch," Sandra laughed, and I suggested we all shared a bottle to discuss the practicalities.

Straight off I advised that they shouldn't begin officially as a club. The backwoods mentality of our local bench being what it was, magistrates would have scuppered them on the matter of a licence before they were down the slipway. Hazard number two was the fire regulations. Once the local chief had been apprised by his masonic or rotarian pals that gays were converging, there'd be a lightning inspection and a decision that the exits weren't up to scratch because a herd of elephants couldn't stampede out sideways if the need arose. It was a group decision that the opening should be a bottle party exactly one month after Chick had inserted a general invitation via a box number in the Gay and Lesbian News-sheet.

With less than a week to go, he was able to tell us that at least a dozen had replied, for the most part giving first names only. When Sandra heard that there were five women among those preparing to slide out of dusty closets around the country, she brightened considerably and offered to get domestic in the matter of baking cakes. The others knocked up sandwiches sufficient to bloat twice the expected number and I set aside a couple of cases of light table wine with the promise that I'd haul them round within minutes of the bar closing. That was a week when we were all busy and blithe with the optimism of late spring.

"So ... what do you think?"

Lennie had taken the cases from me to let me have a better look round.

"Lost for words," I said. And I was. The garden was like mid-day with floodlights borrowed, no doubt, by Lennie from the town hall stores. Subtle music sweetened the slightly chilly night and from every flower-tub and hanging basket great clusters of lavender balloons swayed in the light south-westerly.

Sandra, passing me with a piled sandwich plate, flicked my wrist as I tried to pinch one.

"Get your own bloody food, mate," she said pleasantly and, before I could comment coarsely on her need to watch her diet, she'd dropped gracefully at the feet of a woman I'd spotted from time to time at the farm by the station.

Being what they call the extrovert type – basic requirement in a barman – I tacked around those who were sitting nervously on the edge of kitchen chairs or raised geranium beds. Tony and Frank resented what they felt was my attempt to split them but, as I said, we were in a sense all joint hosts. It was a useful line too with Lennie, whose eyes had doubled their wattage when I arrived in my new white jeans. Since I was heavily into the glad-handing, I never could quite say when the row began.

To this day, Lennie will only admit that Chick chose the end of their one friendly dance to suggest the two of them creep away to put their relationship on a more intimate basis. Why he'd held out for weeks, I don't know. Launch one successful venture first maybe, before tackling the more personal one. All I recall is that when I decided to make a move shortly after midnight, neither of them was around. Everyone else had gone inside by then because of a light shower. Would it had been a cloudburst.

It was just about dawn when I woke, not certain for some seconds whether the thumping was in my head or on my door. Lennie was on the landing, white-faced and unshaven, so I could tell he'd had less than half the sleep I'd had.

"I'll tell you what's up in the cab," he insisted as I was fumbling and grumbling into my tracksuit.

"Look, I don't know how it started, or who started it, or anything. I've been walking all night," he began, his hands waving about in a way that matched his incoherence. He was chain-smoking too as we whirled around the esplanade towards the fishing quarter.

"How what started?"

I pulled another cigarette from his hand and clutched him to me with an arm round his shoulder and the hell with old Alf the cabman.

"The fire ... "

"Christ," I said, "anyone hurt? Chick?"

"Don't know. No one's seen him. I mean the firemen haven't ... "

"You mean they're searching ..."

"No one's injured, but the place is gutted."

An understatement. As we paid Alf off, there was a heavy stench of burnt wood mingling with the smell of a dozen chip shops. Over what remained of the singed lawn, streamers and the charred fragments of balloons drifted in the dawn breeze. The flat was a write-off and flecks of smoking paper (some of Chick's many pamphlets, I wondered?) speckled the wreckage of the club that never was.

Having filched Lennie's cigarette pack and smothered his protests, I fobbed off the fire chief and the fuzz with the suggestion of a smouldering butt dropped at a party. They accepted none of us could help and Lennie's alibi of an all-night walk was underwritten by his appearance. We strolled away, agreeing that Chick was no arsonist. I put it to Lennie that maybe, having been given a personal thumbs down, our idealist trudged off into the darkness, backpacks and all and, had he even noticed the blaze behind him, had ignored it. Lennie shrugged; said nothing.

"It figures. Chick knew that selling news-sheets and running clubs can't finally be enough for anyone."

That last remark I regretted as soon as spoken, fearing that, exhausted as he was, Lennie might ask the same about me and the bar. I followed it quickly with the suggestion that we phone Sandra. She was out but we found her – where else? – at Station Farm. Tony and Frank, when we called them, were far more worried that their neighbours might have heard a car being pushed into the garage in the early hours. Finally, we made our way to Chick's old place. It was locked and had the hollow sound of a home to which no one will be returning.

We turned and looked at each other and Lennie let me know then that he'd not missed my opinion that work and hobbies alone can't satisfy any of us.

"So where do I curl up and sleep from now on?"

He waited and he wasn't going to move until I spoke. Shit, I thought, it's time to be counted. Chick had played everything in his hand. Sandra had Dee. Was throwing in a couple of cases of wine any kind of a bid?

"Better come home for a bath," I said, rubbing a smudge on his nose. "You can borrow some gear until the shops open."

Only the other morning I said to Lennie that going to Sandra and Dee for a meal had become a three year Sunday habit. Alternate weeks they visit us. Frank and Tony never came to the bar after the fire. Not that they ignored us in the street. Then – it must be all of two years now – we had cards from Chick. Each one was a life-guard on a Californian beach. Quite respectable – a nice slice of grilled beefcake but too unsettling for our little grey mice. The error was compounded by Chick, who'd signed each one 'With Love'. Off went Tony and Frank, maybe terrified of the postman, to hunt for a more secluded nest. Of course, they promised to write.

Sandra enjoys winding Lennie up occasionally. Only last Sunday, she was at it as she pushed the cauliflower cheese towards him.

"I found Chick's postcard when I was doing the annual dusting this week. That all-Californian boy had blond hair just like you ..."

"Just like hell. My hair's natural," he protested, but I know him and the two women do too. He was very quiet as he helped himself to seconds. None of us spoke as I refilled our glasses, because we all knew what Sandra was getting at.

STEPHEN AIREY

Messer Rondo

Dedicated to the rest of CADRE: Marc, Christine, Nick, Sean, Tom, Tom, and to Pauline.

"There I was, upside down, on fire, nothing on the
clock but the maker's name ..."
(traditional beginning of RAF tall story)

PART ONE

"You coming along with us, Barden?"

" – Just a minute, hang on –"

"Come on, stop time-wasting — *They'll* be out there waiting
for us!"

"Hang *on!*" Barden called back irritably. Shading his eyes
with one hand, he stared at the bright mass of the school
buildings. Most of the older boys were already drifting off, in
threes and fours: a group of them swaggered past the trees,
talking in loud, adolescent voices, and Barden had to shrink back
out of the way.

"We haven't got all day!" Ellis called.

Barden's intent face broke into a grin of relief. A boy had
appeared on the school steps. He was reading a book as he
walked.

"Sutcliff! *Sutcliff!*"

His friend signalled back, and ran over to the trees. The
other two, who had wandered away to talk about football, rushed
back again.

"We'd better cross by the lowest bridge on the river, then
double back through the woods. There were some of *them*
hanging around by the cafe last week." All four stopped to listen
to Ellis, their acknowledged leader. He was the tallest of the gang,

and the oldest, at twelve years and eight months. His one interest
in life was insects. "Everyone keep a really sharp look-out.
There's nowhere to scatter to till we reach the woods ... Watch
out! What're you –?" A small boy cannoned into the middle of
them, and rushed on into the playground. They stopped to stare
after him, Ellis took two steps towards him, and then they heard
his voice raised in the middle of a cluster of older boys:

"Quick, come on, get moving! They got my brother – Jones.
They were hiding under the bridge and grabbed him. I got away.
Come on, you going to *leave* him?" Shouting drowned the rest of
what he was saying. Four older boys were already racing for the
park, pushing through Ellis's group: the younger Jones headed a
big war-party towards the back gate. Self-appointed messengers
rushed everywhere. More and more groups set off, some
running, some walking, for the park.

"Come on! It's a battle!" Ellis shouted, and the five of them
hurried, half-running, after the others.

Barden stared, heart pounding from the run, at the ten
bigger boys on the top of the bridge, dressed in the blue school
uniforms of the enemy and holding down a smaller, black-
blazered figure on the parapet. Some of the bigger boys from his
side had already leapt the river where it narrowed downstream,
and the rest formed a solid arc at the foot of the bridge. The
enemy were surrounded.

"Think you're big, don't you?" one of the crowd jeered.

"Bleeding *know* we are!" a boy shouted back, and ran
straight at the crowd. He stumbled back with a bloodied nose.
There was a shout of rage from the defenders of the bridge, and
they hoisted Jones up so that his head and back lay suspended
over the blue water.

"Give up," a fifth-year yelled. "You can't get away."

"You come and get us then!" one of the besieged yelled
back. Another quickly added, "You try it on and we'll chuck him
in the water."

"Don't know what they think they're doing," Ellis muttered
to Sutcliff, staring over the jostling sea of black blazers. "If they'd
got any sense they'd run for it before *they* all end up in the water."
Shouts broke out on the other side of the river: someone had
spotted more of the enemy's blue blazers over near the woods. A
hunting party raced off in that direction. "Get them! Get them!"
the crowd howled. The youngest of Ellis's group, a small, freckled
child, stuck both little fingers in his mouth and let out a derisive
whistle at the gang trapped on the bridge.

Now a muttering had started in the main group. "Gardiner," people were saying, "Gardiner." "Gardiner's here," a first-year told Ellis excitedly. The crowd was now swelled with many people who didn't go home through the park. It began to split, to make a passage: and Gardiner, huge, yellow-shirted, and strong as an elephant, paced up to the foot of the bridge.

"Right. You put him down right now. You've got no chance."

The fighters elbowed their way through the crowd, to be with Gardiner if he decided to start anything. The crush at the riverbank began to yell and whistle: then, more ominously, subsided into an expectant silence.

It was broken by loud howls from the woods. About half the hunting party reappeared, running desperately towards the river. Following them came twenty of the enemy on bicycles, riding in formation, like cavalry. The hunters got scarcely half-way back before they were ridden down. More bicycles appeared coming down the road towards the bridge: and a mob in blue blazers emerged from the wood.

"Get them! Get them!" Gardiner shouted, and rushed with his followers up the bridge. Jones wriggled free, escaped falling in by a miracle, and ran down the other side of the bridge to join the flight downstream.

"Come on," Ellis said tersely, "We've got to get out of here, quick. There's going to be a big fight. Down to where I said, then round the long way. Those woods are suicide."

They raced downstream. "Faster," Barden gasped. "They've got no chance back at the bridge. It's only Gardiner holding them."

"The river," Skinner, the smallest of them, said, "will be running with blood."

"Ours, if we don't make the bridge in time," Sutcliff said shortly. Skinner laughed, panting for breath. From the downstream bridge they could see, through the long fronds of the willow, a confused mass of black and blue blazers struggling back and forwards by the narrowing of the river. A few figures struck about them still on the crown of the upstream bridge, but already the enemy were riding swiftly over the hump, in single file, crossing the river. They heard distinctly Gardiner's tremendous roar from somewhere up at the fight, a hundred yards away:

"Run away! RUN AWAY!"

There were shouts of laughter from somewhere nearer. Scattered knots of black in the green expanse showed where

some bands, despairing of getting away, were standing to fight.
Gardiner's advice seemed more sensible than anything taught in
lessons: Ellis forced his weary gang to start running again. They
sprinted for the gap in the woods. Skinner and Bailey, the
smallest, began to lag behind.

"This'll be a lesson to me," Sutcliff gasped, jerking his
briefcase onto his hip, "only to take the books I really need."

"That pond's got diving-beetles in it ..." Ellis said ab-
stractedly. "It's going to be harder than ever to get home after
today – "

The gap was straight ahead. But it was filled with a horrifying
sight: six huge enemy on bicycles were swooping down on them,
riding from the road.

"Go for the woods," Barden hissed desperately. It was
obviously too late: so he muttered again, "If we get a chance,
make a break for the woods."

The enemy rode into the middle of them: one jabbed an arm
out, and knocked Ellis to the ground. Bailey tried to run before
they had all dismounted. Two of them rode after him, threw
themselves from their bikes, and hit him in the face.

"See this knife?" the leader said to Sutcliff.

"Yes, I can see it," Sutcliff said. "Gosh, it's a good one. You
must be pretty brave to carry a knife like that. You're not afraid of
the police at all."

"No, I'm not," the boy said complacently. "I'm not scared of
any pigs."

"Never seen one as good as that before," Sutcliff continued
subtly, pretending to ignore the sounds of Bailey being beaten up.
"It must've cost you a bit."

"Ten quid," the other boasted. He seemed to have given up
the idea of using it. Barden had got the idea. "Is that knob for the
spring?" he asked, gaping with reverence. They had let Bailey go
now, and he and Ellis and Skinner were edging imperceptibly
towards the woods as Sutcliff and Barden played for time. All the
enemy had dismounted now. Ellis turned to Sutcliff and made a
small gesture with his hand: and instantly the five of them raced
for the woods. Sutcliff scooped up Ellis's briefcase.

The enemy grabbed their bikes. They were going to ride
their captives down. In the centre of the formation the biggest of
them, red-faced and grinning, rode leaning back and flourishing
his knife. Ellis's gang was not going to make it into the woods.

Suddenly Sutcliff jumped to one side, pulled Ellis's briefcase
open, and snatched out a large shoebox. He ripped at the

sellotape on it, and taking aim in the manner of a discus-thrower, hurled it like a grenade at the face of the rider with the knife. It burst open: the bicycles swerved wildly and collided, bringing their riders down. They threshed about on the grass, swatting the air and yelping with pain. The five fled into the woods.

"My bees!" Ellis lamented. "My bees!"

"You can't say they were wasted," Sutcliff pointed out. "You can collect some more."

"They're difficult to catch. I had seventy-seven of them."

"I was crying like that," Bailey said, "so's they'd be satisfied with what they were doing. If I hadn't cried they'd have hurt me much worse. I didn't need to cry at all."

"Neat idea," Sutcliff said. They looked at Bailey with respect.

"I'm going to ask my Dad for the bus fare home the long way," Ellis said. "I don't think this way's going to be safe in future."

Sutcliff didn't reply. He had taken his latest book out of his briefcase and was utterly absorbed in it.

"And STAY OUT!"

"They think they're so great," Sutcliff said bitterly, retrieving his briefcase. "Look at him swagger. What did you say?" He stuffed his cap in his pocket and began collecting stray books. Rock music blasted out from the open windows of the music room. The next sixth-form disco was in preparation.

"We had permission to be in there!" Barden glared indignantly, from a safe distance, at the prefect Evans. "*He* threatened to give us an imposition. And *he* was the one breaking the school rules."

"French won't thank him for that," Sutcliff said, pointing at the music master's record of the first Brandenburg Concerto lying bare on a greasy table-top. "Hey Barden, look at that! Frenchie's record. He won't thank them for that."

Barden had retrieved a book Sutcliff had overlooked, and was reading the blurb.

"Hey, what?"

"Hand it over," Sutcliff said hurriedly.

"But it's –!"

The bell rang. "Never mind what's on the back." Sutcliff seemed flurried. "Tell you about it in break." He held his briefcase open to receive the book: and they joined their form in line.

Sutcliff had found the book in the local library. All the children's and adults' books were in one long room, so that adults

could read things they hadn't read since they were young, and
children could, as Sutcliff did, borrow adult books. The librarian
did not seem to notice the difference, if there is one. It seemed to
be a sort of thriller. That night he kept putting off his homework
till it was too late to start: and long after he went to bed he kept on
reading under the covers with the aid of a torch and a snorkel
made from an old hosepipe, which, though he had to admit it
hindered rather than helped his breathing, he was reluctant to
discard absolutely.

"It's the best book I've ever read," he explained to Barden in
morning break. "It's a sort of detective story. It's all about
homosexuals."

Sutcliff, having only recently discovered logic, respected it
more deeply than any adult: and so he had no hesitation in feeling
indignant at the mindless persecution the book described. He
hated bullies. Barden, when he read the book over the next two
days, was more impressed by the heroes than the villains. He
liked the idea of a resistance movement of homosexuals over the
country, constantly defending themselves against violent idiots,
discriminated against by narrow-minded and uncomprehending
authorities, but growing stronger with each new day and never
ceasing to challenge the oppressors who could never entirely
defeat them. The situation seemed to resemble in many ways the
plight of a twelve-year-old boy at school.

"They're just like us," he told Sutcliff in break, when he
reluctantly returned the book.

"Yes, but they're even worse wronged," Sutcliff said. "I
don't see why people pick on them. There's no *reason* to." He
was outraged by this offence against logic. His mum had told him
that sex was an enjoyable and affectionate act taking place
between two people that he would understand better when he
was older. He could see nothing in that definition to stop the
people being two men, or two women. "Something ought to be
done about it."

Barden agreed.

When Sutcliff said something ought to be done, he meant
that he should do something about it. "Well, we ought to join on
their side, then," he said indignantly. "It'll be dangerous," he
added, with vague recollections of parts of the book. "But we'll
have to do what we can."

"That's right," agreed Barden. He liked defying authority
with a lot of other people. Sutcliff liked the idea of defying
authority.

"Ellis," he said, "don't *you* think it's wrong?"

"What is?" Ellis had only just arrived under the cherry trees. It was another hot day. "Do you want to sneak round the cricket pitch? I've got a butterfly net hidden there and you could take turns with it."

"The way that people treat homosexuality," Sutcliff continued, as they set off.

"Homosexuality?"

"You know – men who fall in love with other men."

"Oh. Queers?"

Sutcliff was silent. He had only just realised that "queer" – the deadliest insult in the playground – didn't mean "wrong in the head" as he'd casually assumed, but homosexual. It was Barden who replied.

"Yes. If two men are in love with each other, how are they doing any harm to anyone else?"

Ellis considered the matter. "I shouldn't think they are – not to anyone *else*."

"So the laws against them are wrong," Sutcliff said.

"There aren't any."

"Yes there are. This book I read says so."

"Probably just leftovers," Ellis said, relegating British Law to the significance of a school meal. "Ah, but what about if they try it on with other people, with normal people?"

"Even if they don't, there are still laws against them," Barden said.

"And besides," Sutcliff broke in, "there aren't laws against normal people trying it on with homosexuals, so why should there be laws the other way?" When he said *normal*, it was in a tone of deep contempt. The word seemed to him to have an aura of schoolmasters telling him that *normal* boys ate up all their school dinners. Ellis saw the force of this argument. To him the word brought up visions of jeering older boys telling him that *normal* boys weren't interested in insects.

"Why don't you bring the motion up at the debating society?" he said enthusiastically. "You propose the motion and I'll second it."

"Yes, let's do that!" Sutcliff said. He was jubilant at the idea, which seemed to solve all his problems of what to do next. He was confident of his ability to refute any arguments the opposition were likely to bring up.

"It's another Red Admiral," Ellis said, lifting up the net. "I thought at first it might be something rare."

The butterfly basked for a few more seconds in the hot sunshine, then fluttered away across the cricket pitch. It was the end of the lunch hour; the bell rang.

It wasn't as easy to collect supporters for the debate as Sutcliff had anticipated. The forthcoming debate had become the centre of his life: it was the most important thing that was going to happen, and he couldn't talk about anything else. But to Skinner, for example, it was obvious that the laws against homosexuals were justified: if they weren't doing any harm, why were there laws against them? A friend of Skinner's agreed, pointing out that there had to be laws against homosexuals because they were effeminate "like girls". Bailey said that the laws were justified because homosexuals were in a minority.

"You mean, as there aren't many of them, there should be laws against them?"

Bailey agreed to this, and Sutcliff became angry; but the general feeling was against him, Skinner pointing out that if they didn't want to be persecuted, why were they homosexual? Everyone agreed this was unanswerable, and the point of the discussion was lost when a certain Johnstone accused Sutcliff of being a Liberal, which led to a game of British Bulldogs between the Labour and Conservative supporters present.

Sutcliff was the more angry of the two: an offence against logic seemed a personal affront. Barden, more stolid, had as usual simply followed Sutcliff's lead.

"They won't be able to behave like that at the debate," Sutcliff fumed. "They aren't even producing sensible arguments." Application to his mother had produced a stock of sensible arguments which he was confident of refuting.

"Maybe Evans won't be in the music-room this time," Barden said hopefully. "You can go in and play your Bach."

"Hullo," Ellis hailed them. "The debate's next Wednesday. I'm doing the proposing, you're doing the seconding, Sutcliff."

"I thought I was making the first speech."

"Sorry, it can't be changed now." Ellis scooted off.

"Yes," Barden said resignedly. "It's one of those days." Sutcliff seemed about to say something. "Come on."

"*Damn* sixth-form disco," Sutcliff muttered ferociously.

"It's the Beatles," Barden said. "Real old stuff."

"I can't tell one of these groups from another," Sutcliff replied loftily. "You'd better tell Ellis, he might go in and collect them. That might shut them up." They both laughed.

Bailey was half-way up a drainpipe. His cap was the whole way up, and he was heading up to retrieve it.

"Hey!" Sutcliff called.

"No," he said, "I'm not going to argue with you any more. You've got it on the brain, Sutcliff. Who wants to talk about it?"

"What we were going to say," Barden said meditatively, "is that there's a wasps' nest up there." Bailey had just discovered this. He fell off the drainpipe. What Sutcliff had been going to say was that the debate was tomorrow. He had probably overdone the original advertising. But he was absolutely confident as he walked up the road to his home. He heard the soft thumping of a big drum as he went past one of the turnings off.

"No, look," he heard an impassioned voice calling. "Supposing we try the new ones? There isn't that much time to go before the music festival – Look, we could just try 'Here Come The –' "

"No, I'm not really satisfied with the lyric yet. It needs –"

"Oh, for Christ's sake!" someone said.

It was a wonderful evening. He got his homework finished before supper. He went to sleep in a lucky mood.

"Christians," Ellis said, "may regard it as sinful. I'm personally not a Christian, but doesn't the Bible say, 'Love thy neighbour'? And Jesus stopped people stoning the woman taken in adultery, and that's a sin, too."

"But in any case, as long as these people don't harm members of the public, why should they be punished? They're surely more cases for doctors to deal with than the police."

Miss Carter was nodding approval. She was the teacher who had instituted the Debating Society, and supervised all its sessions.

"It is hardly these people's fault. It's something they were born with. To punish them for it is like punishing people born blind, or deaf. And even if you say they might corrupt other people, so might people suffering from the plague – and you wouldn't put those in prison, you'd put them in hospital.

"I think the present laws against homosexuality are wrong. And I think society's attitude towards them is wrong. They should be able to admit what they are in public without fear of losing their jobs. They shouldn't have to wait till they're twenty-one before they dare meet other homosexuals. Provided they stay within the law, they should be able to tell other people they're homosexual without fear of being attacked; and other people should not treat them any differently for it."

Miss Carter and the regulars of the debating society clapped politely. The mass of others who had crowded in for this debate remained silent. There was some furtive laughter. Keagan, a big, spectacled third-former, stood up to make his reply. Barden, from his seat in the floor of the house, could see that Sutcliff was white and tense – doubtless with the stress of having to follow as good a speech as Ellis's, *and* answer this experienced third-form debater. He shut his eyes: the sun was shining directly in his face.

Keagan stood confidently, glancing casually over the house. Unlike Ellis, he carried no notes, and was certainly not going to make a prepared speech.

"I'm going to start by disproving most of your points," he began. "Then I'll point out some you overlooked: and the 'logical deduction'," he said, in a faint parody of Ellis's style, "I shall draw, is that the present laws do not go far enough."

"You *think* you will!" a first year said contemptuously from the floor. Ellis was the only one in his year to make speeches in the debating society, so he had their support.

"First," Keagan said, ignoring him, "Christianity has nothing to do with the law. If we obeyed the Ten Commandments, we couldn't have an army, and then the Russians would be over here in no time. Surely you're not in favour of that? But in any case, there are many places in the Bible where homosexuality is stated to be wrong.

"You state that as long as these people don't harm members of the public they shouldn't be punished. But that is like saying that as long as a thief doesn't steal, or a murderer go around murdering people, they shouldn't be punished. Homosexuality *is* harmful to the public: that's why there are laws against it. I agree that if doctors can cure the condition in individuals they should: that's one of the reasons why they have doctors in prison. But society is fighting not against just individuals, but against homosexuality itself. It is a fact of history that homosexuality, by corrupting societies from within, has destroyed them.

"And that is why there must obviously be laws against it, as against any other subversive creed. If homosexuals gain control of our society they will try to make everyone else homosexual. They will destroy law and order. They are already trying to change any law that doesn't suit them. Unless homosexuality is stamped out our society is under threat. As you can see, the present society is allowing it to grow. I say that the present laws are not enough. Homosexuality must be made, as it has been throughout our history, a criminal offence."

He smiled at the applauding audience. The crowd at the back began to cheer and stamp their feet. Miss Carter did not seem at all pleased.

"Silence!"

She turned to Keagan.

"Thank you."

As soon as Keagan and Miss Carter had sat down, Sutcliff sprang to his feet. He was white and tense with rage, glaring furiously, his mouth twisted into a sneer.

"*I'm* going to start," he said, speaking directly to Keagan, "by disproving most of *your* points – those that are worth it –"

"Speak to the House, Sutcliff," Miss Carter commanded.

"Then I'll point out some *facts*: then I'll prove that the present unjust laws should be abolished because they are unjust."

A voice at the back of the room repeated: "Unjust laws are unjust", and its neighbours sniggered.

"Silence!" called Miss Carter.

"You haven't proved that homosexuals harm anyone. You say they corrupt them. How do they corrupt them? By tempting them to become homosexuals? How can you be tempted to do something unless you want to do it? And if you want to be a homosexual, you are a homosexual. Anyone who wants to be a homosexual is a homosexual because he wants to be one. So there's no such thing as corruption."

He had lost the audience, who were looking bored and contemptuous. Miss Carter seemed rather dazed.

"And as the only reason you give against homosexuality is that it corrupts society you're wrong.

"But your argument was based on what Ellis said, so you're doubly wrong. Because Ellis is wrong."

"You can't attack your own proposer, Sutcliff," Miss Carter said.

"Sorry, I'm not attacking him, I'm just disproving the points he gave away to the other side."

"You can do that," Miss Carter agreed.

"You've both been saying 'members of the public' as if homosexuals weren't. They are. Ellis said that homosexuals are like people born crippled. They aren't. They're people born different. It's all very well saying they're born with it – *you're* born with it, too – born with – heterosexuality."

Most of the audience didn't recognise this word. A puzzled

muttering arose. Was Sutcliff flinging at them some subtle, incomprehensible insult?

"Different can be better. *Shakespeare* was different. And Shakespeare was homosexual, too!"

A wild cheer rose from the body of the house.

"*Silence!*"

"What difference does it make to what sort of person someone is if he likes other men, or she likes other women?"

They were puzzled again. What was this about women? Sutcliff had done quite a creditable piece of research, considering the sources available. He was particularly pleased with his fact about Shakespeare. He followed up with another of his facts.

"Ten per cent of you are homosexual!"

There was a slight pause, and uproar broke out.

"Silence!" Miss Carter turned to Sutcliff. "You really shouldn't say things like that."

Keagan stood up, out of order. "Sutcliff's told us a lot of 'facts'," he said. "This one can easily be tested. Hands up all homosexuals!"

The crowd laughed happily. No hands went up. Keagan turned to Sutcliff. "Not a single one," he said.

"No queers here," a voice remarked at the back. There was more jeering laughter. Sutcliff realised bitterly that he had lost the debate.

An inspiration came to him. There was one way he could prove Keagan wrong, and wipe that grin off his face. Ten per cent of the hall had kept quiet. Very well: he would falsify the statistics the other way. Slowly, defiantly, he raised his arm.

"*I'm* a homosexual," he said.

In the momentary silence that followed this assertion, Keagan, still smiling, said, "Not a lot of you, is there?"

Another of Sutcliff's awful "bright ideas", Barden thought in despair. He wouldn't desert his leader: but it was much harder for him than for Sutcliff.

"I'm a homosexual, too," he said deliberately, and raised his right arm above his head.

His neighbours drew away from him. Keagan stared at him and said with equal deliberation, "Oh, like that, is it?"

"Be quiet, Keagan!" Miss Carter said furiously, but it was too late. Sutcliff stepped down off the platform as if the debate were over, and Barden followed him. The crowd drew back to let them past. It was a frightening walk. Some of the bigger members of the crowd jostled forward as if to follow them out, but Miss

Carter cried sharply, "Close that door!" Barden and Sutcliff were shut out in the open air. She frowned down at the debaters. "Now we will have the last speech. Then we will have a vote on the matter. Wallace, start your speech."

"We're for it now," Barden said stolidly. He had a rather better idea than Sutcliff of exactly what sort of unpleasantness was in store for them. One sort that did not occur to him, but did to Sutcliff, was that this was the sort of things teachers reported to parents.

"Yes," Sutcliff said defiantly. "We're for it now."

In the afternoon history class there was a continual mutter that drove the history master, normally a mild-mannered man, almost to distraction. It was: "Sutcliff and Barden are queer! Sutcliff and Barden are queer!" It was only by hurtling out of the classroom and down the stairs before the mass of their classmates that they escaped ambush.

"Quick – into the shrubbery!"

Barden followed unquestioningly. When they were safely hidden, he asked, "What're we doing here?"

"Keagan!"

But Keagan didn't seem to be hunting them. They heard him call out to some of his third-form friends loitering near the entrance, "What're you hanging about for? Come on, we'd better get down to the bus-queue quick."

"We're waiting for those weeds."

"What weeds?"

"The queer-boys." They laughed.

"I'm not waiting around for them," Keagan called back contemptuously. "Stop time-wasting!" He walked off.

"We'll wait till Ellis turns up."

Skinner, Bailey, and the rest saw Barden and Sutcliff emerge from hiding, and moved away. "We're going off now," Ellis said.

"What're you acting like this for?"

."The debate was lost, if you're interested. And the idea of a debate," Ellis continued venomously, "is to *discuss* things, not to make public confessions of them. All right, I'm coming," he added to Skinner.

"What's this about –?" Barden began angrily. Sutcliff, quicker on the uptake, mocked Ellis. "And it was you who said that people shouldn't treat open homosexuals any differently!"

"That's a different matter." Ellis turned his back and walked away.

"Well," Barden said, "if we're going to find it difficult getting across the park, so're they. There's only three of them now, and one of *them's* Bailey." Sutcliff laughed, and began to cheer up again.

The persecution that followed was not of the sort that peters out in a few days. They might have escaped by backing down immediately, but that was unthinkable. Like crocodiles, the bullies began to gravitate towards them. Jefferies and Smail would be waiting for Sutcliff outside Assembly.

"It's the queer weed!" Jefferies snatched the cap from Sutcliff's head and tossed it over to Smail. As Sutcliff tried to snatch it back, Jefferies kneed him in the thigh, so that his leg went numb.

"Say you're queer, weed. Say 'I'm a poof!' " Smail said, fixing his pale, inimical stare on Sutcliff. Sutcliff kicked out, but standing on his numb leg, fell, and Jefferies' hand crashed on the side of his head.

"Come on," Smail said, "we're late." They walked off with the cap.

Sutcliff was in trouble for being late at the first lesson, but the loss of the cap was a far more serious matter. He would get in trouble for not having one, and his mother would have to pay for a new one.

"I'm not going to put up with it tamely," he said furiously to Barden. "I'll take revenge on them –" But at that moment, between lessons, Jefferies looked in through the door, threw the tightly-folded cap at Sutcliff so it hit him in the face, and disappeared again. Sutcliff was very relieved.

These were everyday matters. Barden was set on by a gang after school and both his eyes were blacked. Sometimes they were helped: but twelve-year-olds have not learned the art of ignoring unpleasant times, or to regard a minute of help as outweighing hours of misery, so such help seemed very rare, almost miraculous. One day Gardiner marched into a gang that was attacking them and ordered the tormentors away. The two of them were too awestruck to thank him. And another time they were surrounded by a crowd shouting, "Pansies! Queer-boys carry *hand bags*!" Every so often someone would dart forward and strike at them. Barden clenched his fist. They were being driven back against the prickles of the hedge.

"Clear off, you weeds!" Keagan shoved the leader in the chest, and sent him staggering. The crowd slunk away: and Keagan, ignoring the two who remained, sat down to do his

French homework.

"You don't want to mind them," Barden said. "Just don't listen to what they were saying."

"You were going to fight them for what they were saying," Sutcliff reminded him.

"Ah well, that's different. Can't let them get away with it, can we?"

"We can't even stay in the music room," Sutcliff complained, " 'cos they're always in there doing their recording for the disco ... I've got a good mind to put some things they won't expect on those tapes. I'd like to see them dancing to Beethoven." His mind was filled with a glorious vision of the entire sixth leaping and twisting to the Seventh Symphony. Barden chuckled.

"I'm going to do something about it, though," he said. "You wait."

"What can we do?"

Barden walked out from the shade of the trees into the baking-hot playground, and into the middle of the black-blazered crowd.

"Right!" he shouted. "All of you lot are prejudiced against homosexuals. You've been calling me a queer. Any of you ready to try it in a fair fight? Any of you want to prove your ideas in a fair fight? Any of you want to *risk* a fair fight?" He paused, glaring around him, with clenched fists. "Sneaking off, are you? Who's like a girl now? Come on, you little girls! Fight!" He punched the summer air. "Is there anyone in this *playground* ready to fight for what they've been saying?"

Self-appointed couriers dashed to every corner of the yard: groups of children formed a crush of spectators around Barden. A small group started marching from down by the cricket field up to the trees: and from every group that they passed messengers ran to the crowd, telling their friends, "Green's coming! Green's coming to fight Barden!"

Green marched through the crowd, his followers elbowing their way behind him: he walked into the space round Barden, and instantly the crowd rushed into a circle, swallowing up Sutcliff, and leaving only the minimum space for the fight.

Barden lost his challenge within two minutes. He was blindly striking out at the air, and Green was punching him in the face, when Evans forced his way through the crowd and pulled them apart.

"Green, wait outside the prefects' room in ten minutes'

time. Sutcliff and Barden, come with me." They followed him to
the passage into the prefects' room. It was cool and shady here,
and quiet as if they had been in class.

"They say you started it, Barden. Is that true?"

"Yes, it is."

"*They* started it!" Sutcliff said. "They kept getting at us. It
was self-defence."

"I've heard about that," Evans said grimly. "And there's
nothing I *despise* so much as getting at people. They got at me
when I was in the first form, too. They say you're queer, do they?
If they say that again to you, I'll get them for trying to start
trouble."

Barden would not accept the temptation. "What they say is
true," he said flatly. "But I wasn't going to stand their attacking it."

"Oh!" Evans paused. "You want to be careful of that," he
said. "I know it's tempting to take the wind out of their sails by
pretending to be what they say. It's tempting to glory in being
different, and to be as eccentric as possible. But you won't be
happy that way. Look, I'll tell you something. When I was your
age, they kept saying I was mad. So I pretended to *be* mad. It shut
them up, they even became scared of me. I *enjoyed* the
reputation for a while. But you don't really enjoy being set apart.
You have to come to terms with your fellow-men."

"Even if they're in the wrong?"

"They can't always be in the wrong. And anyway, who are
you to dictate to people what's right and what's wrong?"

"The RE master does. The headmaster does. And all of
them out there do. Why shouldn't we?" Sutcliff was giving in to
the temptation to argue.

"That's enough," Evans said. "Now listen. Because I
sympathise with your action, I'm not going to report this. I could
get into trouble for that. But somebody will probably report it. So
if someone sneaks on you, and gets you into trouble, remember it
wasn't me. That's all. You can go now. By the way," he added, "if
they try it on after school, do better than that, Barden. Hit like
this." He punched the air. As they went they heard him call in
Green and give him two hundred lines.

"Miss Carter wants to see you in the staff-room straight
away," Skinner said. Someone had reported them. "It wasn't me
who told her," he said to Barden.

"So the fight started because of you," Miss Carter said. She
was sitting behind the desk in a small room generally used for
interviews. Barden and Sutcliff were sitting in armchairs. From

this they realised the matter was very serious.

"What I don't understand is why you have to go around telling everybody about it," she began. "It is, after all, very common at your age, I fully understand that. It is a *perfectly natural* phase you are going through. It is, after all, difficult to meet girls socially, and it is only natural that you should ... look elsewhere. As I say, I do know about these things, and I realise the exact nature of your relationship."

Sutcliff was, as Miss Carter had often observed in class, very quick on the uptake, but now he was completely puzzled. He hadn't the faintest idea of what she was talking about. Miss Carter had failed to take into account another common feature of twelve-year-olds: a capacity for fierce and completely altruistic devotion to an abstract idea. Adults, even if they don't have a personal axe to grind, generally feel some emotional attraction to their ideals. She did not notice the blank look on Sutcliff's face.

"You may find each other attractive, and of course it is easier between friends, but when you are older you will make friends with girls, and you will find them far more attractive. But don't worry, this phase you are going through is *completely* natural." She smiled. "However, there is no need to defend it in the way you do. It doesn't need defending. And of course you are quite wrong to say you are homosexuals. That word applies to *adults* who behave like that when they are at an age when they should naturally be attracted to girls."

"Unless they *are* girls," Sutcliff said, seeing an opportunity to pick up a point.

"Of course," Miss Carter said, irritated. "I've been talking only about boys because *you are* boys." It was Barden's turn to feel lost. What *was* all this about girls? But he had fully understood what Miss Carter said before, and explained it to Sutcliff outside.

"She doesn't know what she's talking about," Sutcliff said.

"We can't have any more fights, though," Barden said. "She said she would write to our parents if there was any more trouble."

"Let her. I'm not going to give up."

"Yes, but we don't want to get in that sort of trouble. She said we'd have to see the headmaster."

"We're in the right. If they think we're in the wrong, then they're in the wrong. So we shouldn't pay any attention to them. It isn't any business of theirs."

"Yes, but our parents won't only be angry about what they

complain about, but about us doing things to make them complain about us. So if we go ahead and make them write to our parents, we'll be in the wrong."

Sutcliff was dubious: but as it happened, that evening something happened that not only let him escape from the moral impasse, but gave him a marvellous new idea.

"Have you seen this?" he asked Barden fiercely. "Something we should go into action about. Look at it!" He thrust a copy of the local paper at his friend, and stabbed a finger at an article in the centre pages.

WASTE OF TIME AND MONEY

It is an enduring principle, no matter what party is in power, that no issue is too trivial or too ridiculous to waste ratepayers' money on. The council decided yesterday, after a four-hour debate, not to allow copies of the homosexual magazine Gay News into local libraries. It is astonishing that the issue should have been thought worth discussing. The councillor introducing the motion, Mr Stanley Peppercorn, claimed that representations had been made to him by residents of his ward, members of the homosexual organisation EHE. This is the group, apparently, which disrupted traffic in the High Street on Monday "protesting" against the dismissal of Robert Holmes, a self-confessed homosexual formerly employed at St Mary's Primary School. Cllr Peppercorn admits that he is thinking of "taking up the case". What is there to take up? No sane person would consider employing a drug-addict in a hospital, or a rapist as a child-minder ...

The rest of the article was an attack on Mr Peppercorn and was signed *MW*.

"We may have been stopped for the moment at school. But they can't stop us doing things against prejudice outside school, can they?"

"What're we going to do?"

"Write a letter to the letter-page."

"We can't. If we sign it under our own names, we'll get into trouble. And besides," Barden added hastily, seeing that Sutcliff was not at all convinced by this argument, "they wouldn't publish a letter from schoolchildren – not unless it supported what they were saying, or was about animals."

"Yes ... We'll write it under a false name! And I'll type it out, so they can't tell by the writing." This was a good idea. They argued for some time about a suitably adult name, both wanting it to be something uncommon. After a time, they were suggesting such uncommon names that they were reeling about with laughter.

"Hieronymus Turnip," Barden spluttered.

"Comte Hamish von Plantagenet," Sutcliff suggested, "Herr Heinrich Presto. Messer Rondo –" he sat down and choked. "That one's an idea, actually," he managed to say. Barden looked incredulous.

"No, you see, Messer is the Dutch for Mister. So they'll think he's an Italian merchant, settled in Holland, in England for trade." After a second this exotic character seemed real to Barden. He agreed enthusiastically. (Neither stopped to consider if such a person's views would be regarded as relevant in a local newspaper.) Barden practised the signature several times, until he could write, without any difficulty,

Messer Rondo

at the bottom of the letter Sutcliff had typed.

Dear Sir,

I was much distressed and morally offended to see your Editorial of last week. Why should you assume that homosexuals attack children any more than hetero-sexuals? In my adopted country of Holland homosexuals act as schoolteachers and none of the consequences you insinuate have occurred.

Yours sincerely,

Messer Rondo

Barden had reduced it to a fifth of the original length. Both were proud of Sutcliff's efforts with the dictionary, and his attempt to give the letter a foreign air. They put a Dutch stamp on the envelope as well as an English one. It was not published.

"Do you stock *Gay News*?" Sutcliff asked at the local

library ...

"There's another target." The next day Miss Keene, the librarian, was showing to a bewildered library supervisor a note posted in by hand:

> *Stock Gay News in this library or it will be the worse for you. Signed (on behalf of EHE)*

Messer Rondo

Mr Holmes got a letter that cheered him up considerably that morning:

> *Dear Mr Holmes,*
> *Don't give up hope. Fight for your rights. It is unfair and unjust of them to sack you. We have written to the local paper about it.*
> *Yours sincerely,*
> *M. Sutcliff (12)*
> *J. Barden (12½)*

The second letter to the local paper, though correctly signed this time, was also not published.

The heatwave continued. The laburnums bloomed in great showers of yellow, cats lay slumbering in the shade, or rocketed about dementedly on each other's heels. The grass grew almost as high as a child in the wild parts of the common. The sound of drumming hung on the air. ("Look," said the impassioned voice. "Haven't you got that lyric ready yet? We want to have it ready for the end, right, in case the pigs –"). Ants were everywhere. One day Barden nearly saw a lizard. Sutcliff went onto the common and lay down in the pearly grass by the dog-roses, to watch for giant dragonflies and slow-worms, and chew grass-stalks without being interrupted. He composed a threatening letter to Jefferies, signed Messer Rondo. He entertained himself with a daydream of the enemies of liberty, pretending perhaps to laugh, but secretly perturbed at the thought of the mysterious Messer Rondo: of Messer Rondo himself, a cloaked and masked Italian, waylaying the terrified Jefferies; and refreshed, stopped to think what really to do next. Back at the house he made himself a honey sandwich, poured out a lemon squash, and settled down to read the papers.

What he saw sent him straight to the telephone.

"Is Barden there?"

Mrs Barden laughed. "Yes, Barden's here," she said. "Shall I fetch Barden?"

"Yes, please ... Barden? Can you come over to the common? I've found something important ... In an hour? Ok ... See you."

He sat down to read the report again, and study the pictures closely. All in all he read it eleven times, making sure there was nothing he had missed.

"See? They have demonstrations. Our side have demonstrations. Marching through the streets, thousands of them. Look at the pictures! See what the banners say?"

"CHE? ... Maybe it's a different organisation, though. I like *that* banner." He pointed. "Wonder what the badges say?"

"Probably it was a misprint. I wouldn't put it past that editor. Probably it's CHE, not EHE ... it doesn't matter. EHE will frighten them more. They'll think it's a secret society." Sutcliff stopped and then burst out passionately, "See how *brilliant* they are? *Wish* I'd been there!"

Barden felt as if it was his birthday. He stared at the photographs, his heart swelling with pride. "Gay's the word," Sutcliff said proudly, unconsciously plagiarising a banner, "they call themselves, not homosexual. We must remember that ... "
He was in a state of exaltation back at home as he prepared the badges. The air was heavy with flowers, and he had his music on louder than ever before. "Yes, GAY's what we'll call ourselves ... We're going to be free! We're going to be free!" He daydreamed. "They'll have reason to remember the name of Messer Rondo before we've finished," he said grimly.

Messer Rondo was no longer the name of a person, no longer their imaginary Italian ally: it was the name of a Secret Society, and he knew they were going to be famous. He was absolutely happy.

Next day he got on the bus, flushed with nervous pride, wearing his badge twisted at an angle. He enjoyed watching people's heads lapse slowly down on one side so that they could read it, then jolting primly upright again. The bus-conductor read it slowly to himself.

"Well, it takes all sorts," he observed genially. He punched the ticket. "Why, hullo Mr Wentworth! How're you? Didn't see you down on Friday."

"Ah well, I went to that do at Julie's on Thursday."

Sutcliff wandered through the park talking to the squirrels and waving his arms heroically. In morning class he had to be told to take the badge off.

In Assembly for once he couldn't feel Jefferies' grey, snaky eyes fixed on them: but they were. And he forgot to take precautions.

Barden had spent his evening finding out about CHE. He could only read one of the telephone numbers on the banners: but that was enough. He couldn't make out the words above it, but he rang the number.

"Hullo?"

"Oh, hullo ... What is this number? I'm sorry, I mean, who am I ringing?"

"This is Lesbian Line ..."

"Ah. Can you tell me the number of CHE?"

"CHE? What district are you calling from? I suppose you do want the local number, or if you like I could tell you how to contact the London branch, whatever you like ..."

Barden named the district. "CHE *is* a men's group, isn't it?" he said.

"A men's group? It's mixed – " Then suddenly, with a note of suspicion in her voice: "You *are* a woman, aren't you?"

"No, I'm a boy. But I'm only twelve, you see."

"Oh! Well, I'm not so sure that I'm able to help you, then."

"What do you mean, you're not sure?" Barden said furiously, lent unusual assurance both by embarrassment and the fact that he'd been taken for an adult. "We're both gay, aren't we? Or are you?" For a moment there was the terrible fear that he'd got a counselling group and they'd find out who he was. He was tremendously relieved when he heard her say meekly, "Oh! Yes, you're absolutely right. I'm terribly sorry. It's my first time on here. Of course I'll give you the number. Do you want to know about CHE? I mean, what it is, and what it does?" He assented gratefully. She told him everything on her fact-sheet, and they rang off in the friendliest manner ("Maybe I'll meet you at CHE some day," she said); he felt immensely pleased with himself. He had a good deal of facts to give Sutcliff. He was still a bit shaken by his own daring, and this was the first time he had ever rung up a complete stranger, so he decided not to ring CHE that night. There was also something else he hadn't got round to asking. She had told him about a Gay Teenagers group. Did that mean he wasn't allowed to join until he was thirteen?

He didn't get to talk to Sutcliff until he arrived late for the first lesson, with a black eye, but amazingly cheerful.

"Has someone left you a million pounds?"

Sutcliff had walked straight into the trap after assembly, wandering along lost in thought. Jefferies reached out to snatch his cap, a torment he never tired of. Sutcliff hadn't noticed him. As the hand whipped down towards his pocket, he thrust his own hand down quite automatically to protect his cap: and jabbed his nails into Jefferies' hand. Jefferies hit Sutcliff in the face, so that he fell crashing against the wall. Sutcliff rushed forward and butted Jefferies in the stomach, so that the older boy, in his turn, crashed against the opposite wall. Sutcliff, transformed into a small fury, punched him twice more while he was regaining his breath. Smail grabbed Sutcliff by the collar, bursting the buttons on his shirt, and twisted his arm painfully up behind his back. He drew back his fist to hit him in the stomach: but an enormous black hand struck him viciously on the side of the head.

"You've been asking for it, Smail," Gardiner said. "And you, Jefferies," he added, "Piss off."

"They ought to make Gardiner a prefect," Barden said, when Sutcliff had finished his story.

"They won't though," Sutcliff said. "He's always in trouble with the prefects himself."

"They still should make him a prefect."

"Of course they should," Sutcliff said. Then Mr Bennet came in, and the lesson started.

That week, Messer Rondo became a topic of irritated speculation in the staff-room.

"What *is* this Messer Rondo?" Wilks demanded. "I find it on blackboards, on stickers ... Whole classes have taken to chanting 'Messer Rondo' under their breath, if I'm not careful ... There are *paper darts* with this silly message on ... Is it a nickname? Is it your nickname, French, by any chance?"

"No, no. None of my classes even want to know what a rondo is. They think *allegro* is a car. Whenever I mention the word the little toads start going 'Rrrm Rrrm' at me."

"Musical delinquency. Dear God, what next?"

" 'Holmes, a child has done this horrid thing!' " Mr Fish quoted happily, waving his pipe in the air. "But what," he said with a sudden excess of despondency, "if anything, does it *mean*?"

"Something subversive," Miss Carter said. "Actually I have a feeling that the centre of this Rondo nonsense is somewhere in IA – most of the idiocy seems to stem from there."

Sutcliff's blackboard campaign had been a brilliant success. "Messer Rondo" had become a new catchphrase. Sixth-formers would observe, after any stroke of wit, "Rrrrondo!" rolling the R and giving a full Italian zest to the "ondo". Lines and impositions were handed in with the dreaded signature of

Messer Rondo

and Mr French had to give up the use of the word for a fortnight. A letter appeared in the local paper, praising the orderly behaviour of the school – in sharp contrast to recent complaints. It was signed Ron Dough. The headmaster was disconcerted by the wild cheers that broke out when he read aloud the clipping in Assembly. Older boys "rondo-voused" with their girl-friends. And at the end of the week, Sutcliff stood for an hour outside the local library with a sign reading:

BOYCOTT THIS LIBRARY. WE DEMAND GAY NEWS.

He enjoyed his first experience of picketing immensely.

Next week there was a lower-school outing, to an open-air production of *A Midsummer Night's Dream*. Barden and Sutcliff had put their names down for it a month ago, chiefly to avoid afternoon school. The trip also offered plenty of opportunities for rondo-type mayhem. So it was with a feeling of pleasurable anticipation that they walked along, talking to Ellis, at the end of the line filing into the park. Mr Bennet had rushed up the line to deal with a sudden outburst of yells. Barden was eating peanuts.

"So we were going to get some hydrogen balloons," he said, "and then – hey! Stop that!" A pigeon had alighted on his hand, pecked some peanuts out of the bag, and flown away again.

"Do they like peanuts?" Ellis said, interested.

"They like these all right," Barden said aggrievedly. Ellis threw a peanut towards the nearest pigeon. A sparrow took it. Sutcliff was already on his knees, trying to persuade a pigeon to feed out of his hand. The birds also liked crisps. A lively and experimental time was had by all, till Ellis cried, "Christ, we've lost the rest of them! Run, we'd better catch up!"

"Just a minute while I see if this duck's going to feed out of my hand," Sutcliff called back as Ellis set off. Barden was too involved with a circle of sparrows to look up. So it was Sutcliff who saw the boy with a catapult. Instantly all thought of *A Midsummer Night's Dream* vanished from his mind.

"Look at that!" he said in a low voice to Barden. Barden looked: and raced off without a word. Sutcliff followed him.

"What you think you're doing? You leave them alone."

"Drop that catapult," Sutcliff added. His face was twisted into a furious snarl.

"Like shit I will," the boy said. "What's it got to do with you?"

"You're not firing that at any more birds," Barden said, clenching his fists. The boy was about his age and size. He dropped into a crouch.

"Who says?"

"Me."

"Oh, *me*, is it? You and whose army?"

"What you do it for? They've done nothing to you."

"Ok, so what?"

"How'd you like someone to chuck stones at you?"

The boy dropped his catapult back in his pocket. "I just felt like it. You'd feel the same."

Sutcliff suddenly realised that at some time the boy had been crying. Perhaps someone had beaten him up ... "Here, what's the trouble?" he said. The boy was silent. "No need to say. Look, have some crisps," he went on desperately.

The boy ate all their crisps ravenously. "Thanks, mate," he said after a while. "I needed those."

"Have a sandwich?"

He looked at it reverentially. "You've saved my life," he said. He talked as if he were older than them. "I haven't eaten since yesterday."

"There's a cafe over there," Barden said, clutching at straws. "Let's go and have a coke."

Half an hour later the boy admitted that there was no real point to shooting birds: "Though they don't half move if you set a stone up 'em," he added. "I didn't go home last night. Stayed out. What's your names?"

"I'm Sutcliff and he's Barden."

"Have you *got* first names? Or are those them?"

"I'm Martin," Sutcliff said. "And I'm Johnny," Barden added.

"I'm Malcolm."

They had some more cokes for that. "I don't want to see my

mum for a while," was all Malcolm would say about sleeping out. Sutcliff, seeing that Malcolm had said all he would about himself without return, started telling him about school. They told him about the secret society of two, Messer Rondo, and their letters to the paper.

He didn't say much to that: when they asked him what he thought, he said, "It isn't my business." But they got on very well.

"I suppose I'd better be getting home now," he said despondently. "Hey! Look, there's a gay-boy –"

"Where?"

"Made you look!" he laughed. "No, he went down that way. See, him just turning the corner –"

They saw a dim figure whizz round the corner.

"Well," Malcolm said, "best of luck. Cheers, mates. I won't forget this. See you around." He swaggered off towards the road, smoking one of his last cigarettes.

"I don't see how we're going to get into that play," Barden said at last. "Our best chance is to wait outside, and persuade them we've been there all along, when the crowd comes out. Or," he said thoughtfully, "we could do it at the station, and look around in the meantime." It had just occurred to him that he could spend the time in between ringing up, and maybe meeting, the Gay Teenagers group. At any rate he could qualify that point about teens.

"Yes, let's have a wander round," Sutcliff said, evading the issue.

They passed into a long avenue of limes. The grasshoppers were chirping. There was only an hour to go before the play finished. It was very still. Long shadows shuttered the path. In the distance they could see the glitter of some concrete-and-glass building, and the diminished yellow shower of a laburnum. Nearer there was a white sign: TO THE BOATS. Across the park they could hear an occasional clink of glasses, the sound of laughter, and from the other direction a raised voice, picked up and scattered to the air by a battery of microphones, speaking poetry drowned by the sudden rustle of leaves. There was a great shout of laughter. "We'd better go down that way ..." Sutcliff said.

Then they heard a faint rattling noise approaching them, like marbles rolled across a concrete slab. They clambered onto the pedestal under an equestrian statue, stared down the avenue of aged limes to a twin equestrian statue at the far end. "What's that? It sounds like someone racing a pram ..." Barden chuckled. Suddenly, from an unnoticed path, a strange figure shot onto the avenue: it turned like a skier and whizzed up towards the statue. As it approached Sutcliff looked at it with frank bewilderment.

It was a young man, fair-haired, blond-skinned, with a barely perceptible moustache. He was dressed in white gym shorts and yellow-wheeled roller-skates. He wore no socks or shirt. He was carrying a yellow briefcase and a newspaper. And he was skating along at fifteen miles an hour.

"*What* a get-up," Barden said, astonished. They both laughed. The young man, who hadn't noticed them, thinking perhaps that the stone horse and rider were laughing together, went into a skid, dropped his briefcase and newspaper, and righted himself just in time. Barden looked out from behind the horse and nearly fell over laughing. There was another distant roar from the theatre.

"All right, all right!" the young man said. "There's nothing to laugh about. Stop laughing, stop laughing!"

Sutcliff had started being amused now, and couldn't stop. But Barden suddenly went quiet. As the young man picked up his copy of *Gay News* Barden asked him, "Are you gay?" Sutcliff stopped laughing and nearly choked with the shock. Had Barden gone mad?

"I am," the young man said. "And when the revolution comes, it'll be against the law to laugh at people who have skating accidents."

"Is there going to be a revolution, then?"

"No, I shouldn't think so, actually." The young man picked up his briefcase tenderly, felt it, opened it and took out a bottle of wine. "There would've been if you'd broken this," he added. He brought out a glass, examined it carefully, and put it back in the briefcase.

"We're gay too," Barden said. "Only we haven't met any gay people yet until now. Are you from CHE?"

"You make it sound like James Bond. No I'm not, actually. The subscriptions are very high at present." He looked at them. "Are you two playing truant or something? I think I saw a lot of kids in that same uniform marching over to the theatre."

"It was an accident," Sutcliff said. Then he started laughing again.

"What are you giggling about?" the young man said irritably.

"Why do you wear clothes like that?" Sutcliff asked.

"I am what is called a clone. It's a sort of gay uniform ... one of several sorts."

"Not the CHE uniform?" Barden asked facetiously.

"No, it's more in the fashion ... But I'm not a very good clone," he said sadly. "Somehow I can't get the image right."

"It's a very good image," Sutcliff reassured him. "We've been having trouble with our image as well. We've got a Gay Secret Society. It's called Messer Rondo."

"It sounds more interesting than CHE. What does it do?"

"Well, actually, for the last two weeks we've been using it to strike at masters who say things against gays. But before that we sent sinister messages to people like the council. And I stood outside the library with a sign saying: BOYCOTT THIS LIBRARY. WE DEMAND GAY NEWS."

"That sounds like a good idea. *Did* you boycott the library?"

"What?"

"Boycott means not using it."

"No ... you see there isn't another one near enough to go to."

"That's always the problem, isn't it?"

"Do you want some coke?" Barden asked.

"Actually I think I'd prefer to have some of this wine. You don't drink wine? No?" He unpacked his briefcase again and poured himself a glass.

"I'm Barden," Barden said. "And this is Sutcliff."

"Are those your first names?"

"No. I'm Johnny, and this is Martin." He pointed to Sutcliff.

"Pleased to meet you. I'm Ralph." He accepted a peanut. "But what does this secret society of yours, Messo Ronder or whatever, *do*? I mean about your sinister messages – do you carry out the threats? And what people are you threatening, and what for? Tell me more."

It was Martin who explained the origin and purposes of Messer Rondo. Ralph seemed to find the story humorous in places, but expressed a proper indignation when he heard about the editorial. "I think you need to do something about that," he said. "That's the sort of case where you need a secret society. Official societies can only try to reason with him, and it's obvious from what you say that reason wouldn't really work with him. A secret society arriving on his doorstep dressed as chimney-sweeps, or posting frogs through his letter-box, or filling his fishpond with newts, might make him think twice without any blame attaching to official bodies." He drank another glass of wine. "In fact," he said meditatively, "I might do it myself ... what did you say the man's name was?"

"Oh no," Martin said. "We've got to be in on it too. Promise you won't do anything on your own, or we won't tell you the name."

"I could find it out."

"It would be better if we helped you," Johnny said. "We could do a lot more that way. Then there's aliases."

"You mean alibis," said Martin.

"I think my alias," Ralph said, "will be the Lone Clone ... that's how I'll sign my nefarious activities."

"No, why don't you join Messer Rondo?" Martin said excitedly.

"Can I? That'd be good. But I'm still going to call myself the Lone Clone."

"The Lone Clone, member of Messer Rondo ... it sounds good," Martin agreed.

"Martin," Johnny said, "I think the play's already finished."

"What? Oh no! What's the time?"

"Nearly six o'clock. We'll have to rush."

"We'll head straight for the station ... Hey, Ralph! We'll have to meet up again to make arrangements. Can you meet us on the common on Thursday?"

"Only in the evening. I work Thursdays," Ralph said, skating along beside them. "Any common in particular?"

Martin told him which common. "Would eight o'clock be all right?"

"Fine. Right, Thursday on the blasted heath at midnight – or eight o'clock, at least. Hope you get that train. Do you want this copy of _Gay News_ to take along? I've read it."

"_Thanks!_" Martin said joyfully. "Come on, we'd better run, Johnny."

"Just a minute!" Ralph called. "What's the name and address of that editor? Did you find that out?"

"I asked around," Martin called back. "It's Wentworth, and he lives at 81 Acacia Road."

"I've been spying out the land," Ralph said. "I came down yesterday night." Martin and Johnny looked indignant. "No, I'm not going to leave you out. Have you done anything yet?"

"Well," Martin said, "I sent him another letter."

"What did it say?"

"_This is your last chance, Wentworth. Apologise to the people you have slandered, or it will be the worse for you._"

"Ah well, nobody can say we didn't give him a last chance. I've brought along a few things which I think might be useful."

"Tins of *paint?*"

"Wait and *see* ... the trouble is it'll have to be done about midnight, or rather, a good bit later. That's why I borrowed a friend's car, to get back."

"We can easily sneak out after midnight."

"But – "

"Can't we, Johnny?"

"Sure."

"All right, I suppose so," Ralph said. "But be careful. If we get caught we'll end up in court."

"What're we going to do?"

"Wait and see."

"Johnny and me," Martin said thoughtfully, "had an idea it might be to do with frogs."

"It isn't."

"Oh well, we'll use the frogs anyway."

"What?"

"We've got a box full of frogs in my back garden."

"My God."

"And some luminous paint."

"Very good."

"And some pink ribbons."

"What?"

"For the frogs."

"Splendid. In that case the thing to do is to meet up on this blasted heath, really at midnight this time, or rather at half-past one, and wear dark clothes, preferably old clothes. Oh, and bring torches if you've got them."

He was going to go off, but stopped a bit to talk about music and kites. About half-past ten, he said, "Right. I really had better go now. I'm going to fortify myself for this business in that pub I noticed down the road. We'll meet again by this decrepit rose."

"It's not a decrepit rose, it's a dog-rose."

"Woof. Well, I think the occasion calls for a beer. And even if it didn't, I should still want one. See you!"

"Right," Ralph whispered, sliding down to the ground again. "*That*, I think, is about it. You got everything?"

"Yes."

"Is there anything we've forgotten?"

"Luminous paint," said Johnny.

"Nearly forgot. Pass it over, will you? Then get back on guard."

"All clear?" Johnny whispered to Martin.

"All clear."

"That's it," Ralph said. "Let's get moving." A deed of dreadful note had been done.

Mr Wentworth attempted to prise his eyelids open. They seemed to have turned, overnight, into something more in the nature of stamp-hinges. His mouth, too, seemed to have been crammed with some horrible species of gravel. He managed to get one eye open, but at the cost of such an excruciating pain that he recoiled into the bedclothes with a little moan, utterly exhausted.

"Is this consciousness?" he thought. "Thought I recognised it ... There might be something to be said for the alternative ..." A horrible idea occurred to him. At some point during the next five minutes, his alarm-clock was going to go off. He croaked faintly. Possibly if he sprang at the thing suddenly? What on earth had he done last night? His mind seemed to have something to tell him. Something dreadful about socks.

It was at this point he remembered the alarm-clock. He sprang out of bed to neutralise the detonator, but stopped, caught by his image in the mirror. He saw himself reflected in the form of an unshaven, tousle-headed, pallid young man with pink eyes and wearing only underpants. Behind him was a chair piled with crumpled clothes. Behind the chair was a frog.

A frog?

Mr Wentworth turned to look at it. The frog shuddered and closed its eyes.

"I know just how you feel," Wentworth thought, "I know exactly how you feel." He saw another under the table. But why was it wearing pink ribbon? Why did frogs have those horrible, bulging eyes? Why were their toes so long? Why –?

He pulled himself together. "I'm not in the mood," he croaked. "Go away!" The frog glared at him. It had had a late night too.

"Look," he said pleadingly, "I'll count to ten with my eyes shut, ok? ... One, two, three ... Is this a frog I see before me? ... four, five, six ... Or is it but a frog of the mind, a false creation proceeding from the heat-oppressed brain? ... seven, eight, nine, ten, out, out, damned frog!" He looked sadly at the unannihilated frog. "I don't think I want any breakfast," he said disconsolately. He reached for his trousers, turned them the right way out, and gingerly put one leg in. At that point the alarm-clock went off ...

"That pink ribbon doesn't suit you," he told the frog in the hall, picked up the letters from the mat, and let himself out into a horridly irrational world. Life seemed to have turned into something else altogether, and there was no *reason* why ... The triangular facing above his porch had turned pink in the night, and to leave no doubt as to its message, it had also adorned itself with a large blue lambda. The gnomes which normally lurked in the recesses of the garden, to the annoyance of sensitive visitors, were toddling up the path. They bore a miniature banner proclaiming: GAY PRIDE '81. He kicked them out of the way. The same message was traced in the dust on his car. There was something odd about the gatepost, too. He paused to examine it. The number now read:

"*GAY PRIDE '81*", he repeated disgustedly. "I'll *slaughter* the bastards! Those must be the noises I thought I heard about two o'clock. Christ, those must be their frogs!"

The full explanation did not dawn on him until he reached the office, and opened his mail. He had been certain that the parcel he had found wedged in the letterbox would contain something uncanny or odd, and he was not disappointed. It was a miniature Jack-in-the-box, and it popped out at him wearing a badge asking "How dare you presume I'm heterosexual?" and waving a small flag predictably advertising GAY PRIDE '81. It was the unstamped letter that linked these grotesqueries.

Doubtless you have observed our frogs, and bitterly regret your slanderous editorial. Future delinquencies will be more severely punished. Ha! Ha!

"See what I mean?" Wentworth said in the pub. "And this is the Jack-in-the-box." He joined in the laughter.

"You ought to report it to the police, Mike," the tall girl said. She was not laughing. "It's disgraceful."

"Well, it's funny, I suppose. It's given me a good story to tell. I'll be able to dine out on this one. No, of course I'm not going to report it. They'd laugh at me. I can just see myself telling this lot to some duty-sergeant trying to keep a straight face. I'd never live it down. Though," he admitted, "it wasn't so funny to wake up with a hangover and see that frog leering at me. Ever noticed how frogs leer? Ugh."

"I didn't realise queers *had* any sense of humour. They generally just complain all the time."

"Oh yes, I got some very boring, complaining letters when I wrote that article ... Come to think of it, I got a perfectly mad one from the same people."

"You going to write any more articles like that? Remember,

they said it might be worse than frogs the next time ..."

"I don't know what you're all laughing about. It's disgraceful," said the tall girl.

"I'm not writing anything more about that teacher, if that's what they mean," Wentworth said. "He's got another job. But it hasn't persuaded me to read *Gay News*, no." They all laughed again. "You said that article was pompous, Ron – "

"Pompous? They always are," Ron said. "You wouldn't think such pompous articles could possibly be written by a man who, on Thursday night – "

Wentworth blenched. "Hey, er – "

" – took off his socks in order to mop up some spilt beer, then tried to sell them to the bar staff as dishcloths, and then –"

" – Yes, well, *the point is*, I stand by everything I wrote. I can't imagine what could be worse than sharing a hangover with pondlife in pink ribbons," – he shuddered – "but whatever it is, I'm for it now." He turned to the tall girl. "Cheer up, Marilyn," he said. "It's a funny old life. Coming back for coffee?"

At his house, the gateposts were still faintly glowing, as they had since dusk, with the legend: GAY PRIDE '81.

Meanwhile Johnny had a new idea.

"I don't see how I could come in on this," Ralph said. "Even if I thought it was sensible. Is that your kite?"

"Yes. But you will lend me that record you told me about, won't you?"

"Against my better judgement ... This," he said proudly, "is *my* kite."

"It's magnificent," Johnny said enviously. He had got the word from Martin.

"Hullo," said Mrs Barden. "Another kite maniac?"

"Oh, hullo, mum. This is Ralph."

"Hullo, Ralph. My, that's a splendid kite you've got there. Did you make it yourself?"

"Yes, I did, actually. Does it show?"

"No, no, it's just that I'd never seen one like it before. Are you going to be helping Johnny make his pterodactyl?"

"His what?"

"Hasn't he told you about it? He will! It's his great ambition – to build a kite in the shape of a pterodactyl. If you give in to him you'll end up making it, I should think!"

"I like making kites."

"I hope you enjoy flying that one! Don't let him be a

nuisance. Well, I suppose I'd better get on with the supper. Don't be late for it, Johnny!"

During the next week the only activity of Messer Rondo was a secret raid by Johnny, as a consequence of which Mr Wentworth's gnomes started to glow in the dark. Martin didn't know about this: his only activity was arguing with Ellis. Jefferies had stopped ambushing, but still tormented him if he got the chance. The weather was cooler: it rained several times, to many people's relief. Ralph came to tea.

It was on one of those cooler evenings, up on the common, that Johnny revealed his new plan. Martin had for the previous hour been pretending to be a bandit on the run, crawling through the grass. He was covered with raindrops.

"It's the sixth-form disco tomorrow night," Johnny said sinisterly.

"Yes, that's true."

"I think Messer Rondo should take a hand in it."

"*That's* an idea! What sort of hand?"

"I thought a little alteration of the music."

"Beethoven?"

"Not quite ... Also they have stickers to put on people going in. What about printing GAY PRIDE '81 on them?"

"We can't! They'd know it was us."

"Not if we had an alibi."

"They'd still know it was us. Ellis'd catch on straight away."

"So? He couldn't prove it."

"Yes, but he knows what we did to Wentworth, as well."

"What? How did he find out about that? You didn't tell him?"

"Yes, I did ... No, look, it was him I found out Wentworth's name and address from. He lives just down the road. So when he asked about it I could see he knew."

"You didn't tell him about the society?" Johnny was bitterly angry.

"Yes, I did. But I swore him to secrecy." Martin explained the circumstances again.

"You told him about the society? You gave us away? You're a traitor! You shouldn't be allowed in the society."

"*I'm* not a traitor. Ellis won't give us away."

"You don't see, you idiot? Supposing he talks about it? Supposing he gave away Ralph? He'd get into trouble. I'd never be allowed to see him again!"

"You're the idiot. He'd keep quiet."

"Yes, but why did you have to mention Ralph?"

"Ellis'll keep quiet."

"You don't know him. He's like a grown-up some ways. Anyway you've ruined my scheme. Ralph was going to be my alibi but if he knows about this he'll never agree to it."

"He wouldn't have anyway. He'd think it a stupid idea."

"Only because you're a traitor."

"I'm not a traitor."

"You are."

"I'm not."

"You gave away the secret."

"Look, Ellis knew the secret. He'd told me Wentworth's address and next week his house is painted up. The only way to shut him up was to tell him more and swear him to secrecy. It was all I could think of. What would you have done?

"I wouldn't have given away Ralph."

Martin had been feeling guilty about that too. "Look, I'm sorry. But it hasn't done any harm. He won't go back on what he's sworn. All it's done is spoil your scheme, and I'm very sorry about that. Look, you can have my penknife."

"I don't want your penknife." Johnny began to grin. "It hasn't quite spoilt my scheme," he said.

"What?"

"I've done some of it already, *and* I've got an alibi. I sneaked out of Games. You know those tapes?"

"Yes."

"There's a pop-song called 'Glad to be Gay'. I've put it on every tape, in different places. It's on twice in some of them. If they don't want to stop the evening entirely they're going to *have* to play it through sometimes."

"My God." Martin had picked up that expression from Ralph. We're for it now, he thought, but didn't say so aloud.

"It's a pity about the stickers, though." He showed a potato-printer. "I was going to do it with that."

"It wouldn't have worked. You have to have the letters reversed. Otherwise it comes out all wrong."

"Eh? Oh, of course ..." He threw the potato away disgustedly.

"Just a moment, just a moment!" Martin said. "There's something we can put on those stickers." He had recovered his spirits. They had made up their quarrel, but now Johnny, the one who hadn't failed, was more the leader: and it was as a leader that he waited for his lieutenant's suggestion.

"What's that?"

"It won't give us away, but we'll be leaving our signature everywhere. *Messer Rondo.*"

"Rrrondo strikes again!" a sixth-former observed. "Don't go mad, Evans."

"Silly bloody trick!" Evans grumbled. "It's on every sticker. All the girls are bloody giggling at it."

It had been a sultry day, and the last-minute preparations had taxed his patience still further. The air outside was thick with pollen. Greenflies invaded the hall through the open windows. Occasionally a little gust of wind would stir all the curtains, and hot, heavy-scented air would pervade the room. The crickets chirped monotonously outside. The girls were beginning to drift in, in light cotton dresses or in denim, and one or two, straight from school, in a modified version of school uniform; but there were still far more boys than girls.

"Is the bar ready?" Evans demanded. The "bar" served only coke. He could have done with some beer. "Are *you* 'Messer Rondo'?" a girl asked, and moved away giggling, fortunately before he could answer. Fallen pink blossoms rustled on the ground outside. The white curtains twitched in the uneasy air. On the common, dog-roses shed their petals on the wavering grass. The air shifted fitfully in its hot slumber. In the same way the girls drifted petulantly about the room, like so many flower petals, while the boys clustered into groups.

"Haven't you got that equipment mended yet?" Evans demanded. "Come on! Come on! People are getting annoyed!"

"Don't go mad," the amateur electrician observed maliciously. "It's about ready." Secretly he switched the speakers up to maximum.

"What is it?" Evans called across the room.

"It's a weed at the door," the door-keeper called back. "Says he's got to see you."

"If it's an imposition, tell him to come back tomorrow!" Evans shouted. "Isn't that ruddy thing ready yet?" he asked the electrician.

"It'd be ready now if you didn't keep on interrupting. Only a second."

"He says it's important. He's got to see you," the doorkeeper called.

"Who is it?"

"Right, ladies and gentlemen," the electrician announced over the mike. "Sorry about that little delay, but it's all fixed now and - "

"_Bailey!_"

"All right, all right, I'll see him." Evans marched over to the door. "This better be important," he said.

"It's your music - your tapes," Bailey said. "There's something wrong with them."

"And now for the first record of the evening, boys and girls-"

"Someone's got at them. I heard -"

"Sacrifice in 'I Wanna Give You My Love!' "

"SING," a gigantic voice roared, "SING IF YOU'RE GLAD TO BE GAY, SING IF YOU'RE HAPPY THAT WAY, HEY! SING -"

"What the HELL'S that?" Evans yelled. "Is that what you mean?" he said quickly to Bailey. The tape stopped.

"Yes, I heard them say it was on every tape in different places. And sometimes two or three times."

"What, that?"

"Yes."

"Well, now for the _real_ first record of the evening -"

"Who?"

The first drops of rain fell outside: heavy drops splashing hugely on the dusty ground.

"Sutcliff and Barden."

"I might have known."

"IT'S A NEW SENSATION," the tape sang, "A FABU-LOUS CREATION ..."

There was a terrific clap of thunder. Torrents of rain hurtled at the windows, and into the room. The curtains were drenched in seconds.

"SHUT THOSE WINDOWS!" Evans bellowed. "You sure about it?" he demanded of Bailey.

"Well, they've done it, haven't they?"

"Right, I'll see them in the morning. I take it you don't want your name mentioned." He looked out at the lurid sky. "You can't go home in that," he said. "Do you want to stay here?"

"_Can_ I?" Bailey's eyes shone. "That would be super!"

"Sit down there and keep quiet - remember, you're not supposed to be here. I'll bring you over a coke." Evans was more kind-hearted than some of the other prefects. The tape ended.

"SING -" the next song began.

Martin and Johnny were out of luck.

PART TWO

An hour after dawn, the walls of the house opposite were washed with gold light, and the pine-needles on the branch over the roof were brushing before an empty blue sky. There were several things to be happy about, Johnny thought – but then he picked up his wristwatch from the bedside table, saw it was only six, and went back to sleep at once.

Martin woke from gloomy dreams he could not remember, and was relieved to find it was all over. It was the first day of the holidays, and there was nothing more they could do to him, there was nothing they could do about that.

He had supervised the lies they told, he had invented their story. Yes, they had been talking about the alterations to the tapes. So had everyone. It had been common knowledge, a popular rumour. He couldn't remember where he'd heard it. Barden had heard it from him. Of course everyone else disclaimed knowledge of the rumour – what did they expect them to do? It had come down to a question of proof. They knew it was them, but they couldn't prove it. They had punished them as severely as they could on the charge of not warning the prefects of what they had heard; but Evans had not given up the investigation, and had sent for them again and again, checking over their story. They had got away with it now, though. They had got away with it. He went back to sleep.

"You know we'll probably be out when you get back tonight?" Martin's father said. "The key's in the usual place."

"I hope it's going to be good," his mother said.

"Well, the reviews sounded promising."

"I don't know what film we're going to," Martin said.

His father glanced at him. "We're talking about the play we're going to see, not your film."

"I know," Martin said. "I was just saying I didn't know what it was. But we're going to a museum in the afternoon."

"Well, have a good time."

"Lead off from this end!" the man with the red rosette was bawling.

"I don't know how you argued me into this," Ralph said. "I must've been mad."

"We'd've gone on our own otherwise," Johnny said. The procession got under way. A nun whizzed past on roller-skates.

"Look at that one!" Martin gasped, helpless with laughter.

"Hold on," Ralph said. "You laughed at my clothes originally." He was dressed up in his clone uniform again, with the addition of a big leather belt with a huge purse on it. Out of the mouth of the purse a white head peered enquiringly.

"What's that?"

"That? It's my white rat, Tonto."

A little man dressed as a court jester danced by, playing the fiddle. He was covered with badges from head to foot.

"Do they sell badges here?"

"I'm sure of it. We'll find some in a moment. Look, there's your local group coming up behind us." Johnny and Martin proudly watched a huge banner, with the name of their suburb spread across it, marching nearer.

"Do old Wentworth's gnomes still glow in the dark?" Martin asked Johnny clearly.

"Was it you did that?" a bannerman, whom they recognised as a local sweetshop assistant, asked.

"Yes, it was us."

"Great! We were wondering about that. We chased him down the road dressed as nuns the other day. He ran for it."

"He'll be a persecuted minority himself soon."

"There are more of the police than there are of us," Martin said.

"It's always that way," someone said, looking curiously at Martin.

"I don't think we did paint his gnomes, did we?" Ralph asked Johnny suspiciously.

London was washed clean by the rains. Sunlight glittered on wet tiles, on tall sheets of glass and the transparencies of towering buildings, on stone statues and the high yellow wooden paths of scaffolding. The sun shone out of sky-blue puddles and fountain-pools. More and more people joined the march: the wet blue pavements reflected successively a thousand people with tall waving banners. Someone beat on a great drum, the steel whistles of the clones sounded continuously, an unintelligible chanting started at the rear of the column. A church bell began to ring.

"There must be three thousand of us here," the woman in front said.

"The papers'll say two hundred," her companion answered.

Fountains showered ahead against the blue sky and a yellow stone colonnade, the traffic was louder, shouts blew back from the leaders of the column: there was a square ahead. Martin was still half in a dream, and stared at London all around as if it

were a picture gallery of old, wonderful buildings built of stone the
colours of woodsmoke, their outlines whetted by the sunlight, and
in the channel between a stream of people with sundrenched flags
and banners, drums beating, and pigeons cooing in the cornices.
He was marching now past huge flags of all nations fluttering at the
top of white poles on a green lawn: and the brave whistling went
on all the time.

Johnny was looking at the people all around. A tall young
man, with silver-blond hair and a dyed violet bar at the fringe,
waving and twisting a flag so it fluttered in the breeze; a suntanned
girl with a black curtain of hair blowing before her blue eyes,
clutching with both hands a huge sheaf of newspapers; a dignified
old man with a white moustache; three young women, one with a
Japanese paper umbrella; a man with sandwich boards front and
back reading: THE BEGINNING OF THE WORLD IS NIGH.

"Hullo dreamboat," a young man said to Johnny, "doing
anything tonight? Ahhh!" Ralph had skated up and blown a
piercing blast on his whistle right in the man's ear.

"Ahhh! What's that for?" the man repeated, rubbing his ear.
"Oh, I see. You're –"

"Hullo Ralph, or is it Patrick?" another man, in a grey suit,
asked, neatly moving between them. "Or Colin or Joe or Ken? I
can never tell one clone from another. Do you know, Ralph," he
said, drawing the three of them ahead of the fermenting young
man, "there's another clone party tomorrow giving prizes for the
least original costume?"

They slackened pace again. "We've got a fine day for it
anyway. I hope we're not going to walk too far."

"That's typical of you, Slumberland," the other young man
said. His ear seemed to have recovered. "Back at the flat we call
him Mr Slumberland," he explained to Ralph and Johnny.
"Because he's asleep all the time, like a dormouse or something."

"My paternal grandmother," Grey Suit said placidly, "was a
dormouse of unimpeachable pedigree ... But my maternal
grandfather was a Japanese waltzing mouse! I can be very
energetic." He turned to Johnny and Martin. "Do you two want
badges? What are your names, by the way?" He passed over two
lambda badges, which they seized eagerly.

"I'm Johnny and this is Martin."

"Pleased to meet you. At college," he added, "they call this
young man Verloc. Verloc, or the Mad Bomber." He indicated
Ralph.

"*Verloc?*" Martin asked in bewilderment, looking at the

blushing Ralph. "It sounds like something out of *Lord of the Rings*."

"It's the name of an anarchist. Out of a Conrad novel. One day Ralph decided to make some home-made wine –"

"Your name is pretty silly, too," Ralph said desperately.

"– and blew a hole in the floor, covering his tutor with dark red gunk. It was like a horror movie. At least you admit my name's pretty."

"Look!" Johnny said excitedly. "Policemen's helmets! Shall we –?"

"No!" Ralph said. "You're not having one!" They passed by the souvenir stall.

"That," said Grey Suit, "is an idea." A look of holy exultation flitted across his face. He moved towards the stall. The chanting got louder. There seemed to be more policemen than ever.

"What is his name anyway?" Martin enquired. "Grey Suit's?"

"Thorfinn Erik Thorfinnson," Ralph intoned.

"Also known as Erik the Bed," Grey Suit's flatmate said. "I wouldn't put it past him to be asleep on his feet now."

The chant was taken up by the woman straight ahead:

"2-4-6-8, HOW D'YOU KNOW YOUR WIFE IS STRAIGHT?

3-5-7-9, LESBIANS ARE MIGHTY FINE!"

Martin joined in enthusiastically. The policemen scowled. The man with the sandwich boards stopped eating a ham sandwich to join in himself.

"LESBIANS ARE LOVELY!" a woman yelled from a car on the other side of the road.

"THREE CHEERS FOR THAT SISTER WITH THE RIGHT ATTITUDE!" one of the women ahead shouted. The cheers seemed to rock the street. Pigeons fluttered up in alarm. Martin seemed to have lost all his shyness. He had moved ahead and was talking with the women. Somehow he had more badges than before. A woman was sitting back in a sports car immobilised in the stream of traffic on the other side of the road. She winked at the group of women Martin was with, and shouted, "Gays are great!" as the traffic started to move.

"THREE CHEERS –" the cheerleader began.

"Who was that?" Martin asked Annette, the woman next to him. "She seemed to know you."

"That was my mum," Annette said.

Now they were marching between dark-blue double rows of

police on both sides. "Move along! Keep moving!" One of the police, with a flat cap like a postman's, was shouting orders. They passed a big dark-red building with a great arched entrance like a school. On the other side there was a big expanse of grass behind spiked railings, and flowering trees and a long avenue in the distance. It was the park where Martin and Johnny had not gone to the theatre: so they were not yet north of the river.

"Look!" Johnny said excitedly. He pointed to a banner behind them. "It's the Gay Teenagers!"

"Just a minute," Ralph said. They were turning away from the park onto a main road, and the police were keeping everyone in line. As they came onto the road, the floats from the rear of the procession, diverted by another route, came out of a side-street. The drum started up again, and more and more whistles began to shrill. Someone set a football rattle spinning.

"2-4-6-8, HOW D'YOU KNOW YOUR WIFE IS STRAIGHT?

3-5-7-9, LESBIANS ARE MIGHTY FINE!"

"It's all right, Tonto," Ralph murmured reassuringly to the rat. "It's all right. I oughtn't really to have brought you along," he said worriedly. The rat went back to sleep, somewhat like Thorfinn Erik Thorfinnson. The march stopped.

Policemen milled around, pushing the marchers back. "Stop! Move back! Not you!" the man in the flat cap shouted. "Move on after this line!"

"The march goes on!" yelled someone too far away to see what was happening. "In a minute!" a policewoman said to Annette. "Do as you're told."

The floats were being directed into the centre of the march. The last one, immediately ahead, had HEAVEN and ULTRA-DISCO plastered all over it, and the Heaven barstaff inside, naked to the waist, wielding roaring rattles and beating on a gigantic drum.

"2-4-6-8-" the cheerleader began, as the procession began to move again. The drum boomed. Johnny inflated his lungs and screamed out, "1-2-3-4-5-6-7, ALL GOOD CHILDREN GO TO HEAVEN!"

A wild cheer rose from the Heaven float. The edge was thronged with grinning faces. A middle-aged man standing by the drum took up the cry. There seemed to be an odd echo effect, as there had been in that long avenue dominated by two equestrian statues where they had first met Ralph. Some of the gay teenagers were taking up the slogan.

"Slogan," Ralph was telling Martin, "is an Irish word meaning war-cry."

Martin was in a state of exaltation. The music in his mind was mingling with the whistles and the huge chatter of conversation and the sound of traffic and cooing pigeons. The martial air about the crowd was far from being all imagination. Many of the people round them who had seemed to be in entirely carnival mood had vanished, and they found themselves surrounded by grim-faced men and women, marching faster. A helicopter droned overhead, glittering in the sunlight, flying the length of the street.

"GIVE ME A G!" a man bawled.

"G!"

"GIVE ME AN A!"

"A!"

"GIVE ME A Y!"

"Y!"

"WHAT'S THAT SPELL?"

"GAY!"

"WHAT'S THAT SPELL?"

The policemen were beginning to pack the marchers closer together. Martin could no longer see the float.

"GAY!"

"WHAT'S THAT SPELL?"

"GAY!"

"WHAT IS GAY?"

The banners billowed in the wind. Gold and silver letters flashed in the sunshine. The whistling died down for a moment, then redoubled.

"GOOD!"

"WHAT ELSE IS GAY?"

"ANGRY!"

There was a great shout from the front of the column. The march stopped.

"Oh, there you are, Martin," Ralph said. "Where the hell's Johnny got to?"

"Stay where you are!" a policeman shouted.

"I don't know," Martin said. "I thought he was with you."

"What's happening?" Ralph asked a policeman. Annette smiled cynically. The policeman ignored him.

"It's all very well," Ralph said savagely to Annette, "but I'm supposed to be looking after them." The shouting drowned out whatever else he said. Police started running to a point about a dozen yards ahead. A banner dipped and fell. A woman started screaming. Two more banners wavered.

"Where the hell's Johnny?"

"I think there's going to be a battle," Martin said. Ridiculously, he clenched his fists. He was not afraid.

"That's right, kid," Annette said. "Maria! Where are you?"

"But what *is* going on?" someone asked the old man with the white moustache, who had come up again. Ralph was peering back, trying to see Johnny, somewhat hindered both by his height and by not being able to stand on tiptoe with roller-skates on. A girl sat on the ground and began to eat an orange. The whistling had stopped altogether. Many of the policemen were filing away towards the front of the march. There were more angry shouts to the rear, dying down after a minute. Somebody ahead with a strong, clear voice, too far away to be intelligible, began to make what sounded like a speech.

"All right," the policeman with the flat cap said. "You can get moving now. Get them moving," he said to a tall man in a windcheater, with a steward's rosette. The man started striding back along the line. Clones with roller-skates whizzed back down the crowd, spreading accounts of the trouble ahead. Ralph, reluctantly followed by Martin, moved back to try and find Johnny.

"Where did you get off to?"

"They said I can't join yet," Johnny said. "I'll have to wait until I'm a bit older. Hullo, Tonto." He stroked the rat.

"*Seven people have been arrested.*" They could hear the speech now. A woman was sitting on the back of a stone horse. A huge crowd was standing with linked arms all round the statue. The march was being filed round the opposite side of the square. "*The march must stop here! Police back down!*" The police moved in on her protecting screen, and started picking people out of it, apparently at random. There were six police to each arrest. "*Eleven people have been arrested!*"

The march stopped again. Another banner dipped and went down. The whistling suddenly redoubled and chanting started up again.

"*Bloody* police," the man with the sandwich boards said. "We're never going to get there at this rate."

From far ahead, down the street, a megaphonic voice shouted, "MARCH ON! MARCH ON! BREAK THE CORDON! REMEMBER STONEWALL!"

The woman slid off her statue. "*Break the cordon!*" she

shouted. "*They can't stop us finishing the march!*"

"REMEMBER STONEWALL!"

"*Remember Stonewall!*"

"REMEMBER SAN FRANCISCO!"

"What happened there?" Johnny asked.

"A riot – a big riot," Ralph said. "Quarter of a million gays on the streets."

"A battle," Martin corrected him.

Hundreds of policemen were racing by.

"THE CORDON'S BROKEN! THE CORDON'S BROKEN! THIS IS THE FIRST TIME IN BRITAIN –" The voice stopped.

"Yes, but here we're outnumbered. Hell, now we're for it!"

The march had lost all coherence. Most people were milling around aimlessly: the sandwich-board man, followed by twenty or thirty others, was sprinting down a sidestreet against five police who were trying to hold the way.

"THE BEGINNING OF THE WORLD IS NIGH!" he shouted. "THE BEGINNING OF THE WORLD IS NIGH!"

Three helicopters circled overhead. Pigeons fluttered everywhere. A square of people, marching back down the street, began to sing:

"*Freude, schöne Götterfunken*

Tochter aus Elysium

Wir betreten feuertrunken

Himmlische, dein Heiligtum ..."

"Come on," Annette said. "There's one thing better than presence of mind in a crisis, and that's absence of body. Head for the alley there. We'll try and join up with the others farther up."

They moved quickly and casually down the as yet empty alley, Ralph in front, to hide his uniform from the police.

"*Oi! Stop!*"

"Rats! We've been seen! Quick!" Ralph skated ahead into the next road. "Come on! To the right!"

They ran. Maria stumbled and fell. The policeman ran forward, grinning, and Annette stopped, ready to rush back. "*Stop!*" Martin gasped. He turned round: suddenly the policeman's helmet jumped forward over his face, he tripped and staggered into the wall. "To the right!" Martin said to Annette and Maria. "This way!"

"What was that?"

"Messer Rondo!" he called exultantly.

"Messer Rondo and the Lone Clone and Tonto!" Johnny

shouted from round the corner.

"*A policeman's lot*," the large crowd at the end of the street was singing hopefully, "*is not a happy one –*"

"What's happened to the traffic?" Maria asked.

"Oh God," Ralph said. "They've cordoned the area off."

Two large minibuses full of police arrived, one at each end of the road.

"We're all for it now," one of the crowd said.

"Let them come," someone boasted.

"I don't fancy being done on any charge they want to dream up. And I don't fancy waking up in Casualty being told I resisted arrest. Come on! Let's get out of here!"

"Make a break!" someone shouted, and it was taken up: "*Make or break!*"

The crowd surged towards the end of the street: the minibus had not yet unloaded.

"There's no way we're going to get out," Martin said quickly. "We've *got* to make a diversion. Quick! This way!" They huddled against the wall of a great tenement building, part flats, part offices.

"You don't happen to have any bees on you, Martin?" Johnny asked. Martin laughed. "Tell you later," he said to Annette. "Right, watch this." He pulled a steel catapult out from his pocket and shot directly at a jeweller's window opposite, so furtively they hardly realised he'd done it. The glass didn't break: but the alarm started up, and a man rushed out, saw the struggling crowd, and without bothering to look at the window screamed out, "THIEVES! THIEVES!"

"In here," Martin said, and shot in through the office door.

"So that's why the policeman's helmet fell off," Annette said.

"Christ," Ralph said, "I thought you said you'd promised your mum not to get into any more trouble. Heaven preserve me from being with you when you haven't promised!"

"I did. And I didn't want to break that window." Martin was very upset. "That's why I didn't shoot hard enough. But that was the only way of keeping *out* of trouble. I couldn't think of any other way to get them to look away from us." He remembered that at the moment he was leading the party. In a much less uncertain voice he said, "Come on! Upstairs!"

And so, peering from a first-floor window, they saw the last stand of the cordon-breakers: saw the police rush in, hitting out and kicking, and the crowd fighting back with fists, nails and boots: saw Thorfinn Erik Thorfinnson, sleepy no longer, with a plastic policeman's helmet on his head, sparring like a boxer until he went down and was dragged away. The suntanned girl stood with her arms folded and a look on contempt on her face: three policewomen pulled her into a van. The last to go was a young woman wielding a pole crowned with the shreds of a banner; her voice drifted up to them: "GAYS ARE ANGRY! GAYS ARE ANGRY!"

"We had better," Martin said, "try to sneak out by the fire-escape."

"There should be one," Ralph agreed.

It was as they slid off the low flat roof of a Chinese restaurant that they realised they had not escaped yet. It was Ralph's costume that gave them away. A whistle shrilled: and three or four police started pounding up the street towards them, elbowing their way through the startled shoppers.

"That bus," Martin said briefly. They ran. Ralph, Annette and Maria made it: but the bus was drawing away too fast for the boys.

"No!" Johnny called despairingly. "*Don't* jump, Ralph, there's no point –"

The conductor pulled Ralph back from the platform. "You'll kill yourself, mate!" he said, "with those skates."

Martin looked desperately up and down the street. There were more police at the end. Suddenly a voice spoke in his ear. "Quick, mate," it said. "Put this on. Quick, Clive, get your blazer off." Martin and Johnny, not understanding what was happening, put on the blazers and caps. They found themselves hidden in a group of schoolboys their own age.

"Right, you –" the policeman said. "Hey, this isn't them."

"That's right. It's not them." The second policeman stared down at the two white-shirted boys. "You seen anything of a couple of lads, about your age, with jeans? Pelting down this street, they were, about two minutes ago."

"One of 'em with dark hair?" the bigger of the boys said. The policeman nodded.

"Think I saw them get on a bus, over the other side of the road. That one right down there, right?"

"Shouldn't you be wearing a blazer?"

"Left it behind at school. It's a hot day, isn't it?"

"And it's useful if you don't want people to know what school you come from, eh – what's your name? Eh?"

"Malcolm Green."

"Well, Malcolm, if I was you, I'd keep my blazer on. You never know, somebody might ask you to prove who you are." He spoke into his radio, quite audibly, for their benefit: "Finished questioning a suspect, Sarge, where d'you want us?"

"Bloody cops!" Malcolm said bitterly when they'd gone. "What were you doing, anyway?"

"Thanks, Malcolm."

"It was Messer Rondo," Johnny explained.

"On the big time, eh?" Malcolm said as they handed back the blazers and caps. "Good for you. It wasn't that demo, was it?"

"Yes."

"Demos are bloody death, mate. I had a brother end up with stitches all over at one of them. Well, look after yourselves. See you again !"

"There you are," Maria said as they sneaked round the corner. "Ralph's worrying himself sick. Annette's got him hidden in an ice-cream parlour just up there and she's having to stamp on his toes every ten seconds to stop him from running out to look for you. I like him. He's all right. What flavour ices do you like?"

Ralph was disguised in Annette's mackintosh. "There you are," he said.

"Well, at any rate we're safely out of it," Johnny repeated, demolishing the base of his ice-cream with one manic lick.

Ralph was never despondent for long. "Yes," he said, cheering up. "Thanks to Martin. I think, though, we should get right out of this area, soon as possible. Someone might still recognise us."

"Where to?"

"Back home, I suggest," Ralph said, startled. "Where else?"

"Where was the march supposed to end?" Martin asked.

"Hyde Park Corner," Annette said.

"Well, we'd better go there then," Martin said. "Find out what's been going on, and what we're supposed to do next."

"Jesus," said Ralph, in a tone of incredulous horror. "Yes well, that's just typical of you Martin." Johnny too thought there'd been enough excitement for one afternoon. But Martin and Maria were determined not to abandon the march while some part of it might still exist. "Mad," said Ralph, as he gave in. "Mad. We're all mad you know."

What Martin and Johnny did not yet fully appreciate was that the police were far more formidable opponents, both in detecting criminals and in producing appropriate evidence against them, than the authorities of their school.

"Through here! Through here!" Johnny hissed.

"Where's Ralph? Did they get him?"

"No. I don't know. *Down!*"

"Maybe they won't notice the window's open," Martin whispered after a while.

"If they do, they'll be straight through it quick as lightning. Down, down, down!"

"It's car headlights."

"We'd better move back."

"Yes. This way. Did you see what happened to Ralph?"

"Last I saw he was scooting off with two cars after him. What happened to Annette and Maria? You were with them." .

"Stairs! Let's get up them – quick! Hey, I hope the owner doesn't live over the shop –"

" – Who cares?"

"They got Maria. Annette went after her, and I don't know what happened –"

" – Down, *down!*"

The white bars of light spanned the area between the dusky windows and the far wall: dissipated as they turned, and vanished. It was already twilight, much earlier than it would have been on the common. The two boys continued to crouch in that shadowy room full of white and gold roses, cornflowers, irises and dwarf palms. The glass of the open side window was not as clear as that of the huge front windows. The entrance had been too small for any but children. In London, where an unlocked window is as rare as a blue moon, no one but them, probably, would have thought to try it.

"I'm going to close that window. Someone might see it."

"Martin, no! We're going to have to get out that way –" But Martin was already snaking his way between the dusty flowers, and reaching up, too clearly visible in the gloom, to let the window almost noiselessly fall back into place. The flowers rustled round him as he came back.

"Neat work," he said, approving of himself. "We'd better lie low in here till it's all clear."

Johnny had a vague thought to the effect that this was not a game of Hide-and-Seek, and that they might get away with bluff on the street, or they might not – but it was safer there than crouching in someone's shop. But the strangeness and excitement of this refuge made it seem inevitable, if not sensible. He sat down on the stairs. "If you hadn't been so keen on finding out what happened to the rest of the march –"

"What?"

"If only you and Maria hadn't stopped to write on that poster, we might have got away."

"True enough. But it'd got to be done." Martin spoke curtly and absently, as if interrupted in a daydream. He was luxuriating in the feeling of hiding. The room was a square pool of shadows filled with flowerheads. It was like those wasteland sites full of wild flowers and bushes, tanks of twilight air where there had been houses; which would, like the common, be a more interesting place to hide than this. Maybe they could hide in one later on. But this place was still good. He smelt the dusty perfume, sighed, and realised he had been happy without knowing it – which seemed to him a sophisticated thought worth remembering.

"Hey." He shook himself out of his dream. "I've got an idea. If we disguised ourselves –"

Johnny looked pitying. "You thinking of making a false beard out of these flowers?" He shook his head. "You know, we could have found out what happened to the march from Annette's transistor –"

"How would it know?"

"Don't muck around. We could have put on Capital Radio or something."

"But would it have fitted us?" Martin started laughing madly. Johnny fell off the stairs, and rolled about. "Would – shhh!"

They could hear, quietened by the glass, the sound of urgent voices outside the window.

"Keep down!" Martin whispered, peering. "There are hordes of people out there!"

"What's going on?"

Martin peeped out again. "They're all outside the theatre."

"Then we'll never get out of here."

"No," Martin agreed. "We'll have to see where those stairs go –"

The crowd outside had settled down, chatting, in no hurry to go. It would have to be the stairs. The first steps creaked alarmingly. What if the owner lived up there – waiting? They passed a room full of wreaths – lily wheels, scarlet crosses; and halted on the second flight. A blank board barred their way, from floor to ceiling. Judging by the holes punched in it, it was no more than polystyrene.

"I'm going to see where that goes," Martin said.

"No! We'll get caught –" It was only the completely false sense that there would be no turning back that made Johnny follow him. There was a name in lights outside the theatre that

Martin was trying, unsuccessfully, to unravel in his mind, and track down the hidden familiarity. Something to do with today, he decided: had he seen it on the march? He shook his head in irritation. They were going downstairs now, Johnny in the lead again, and at the end of a short, unlit passage they saw, protruding from a quarter-open door, a tiger's head. The dark room beyond was filled with masks and paper flowers and old woodwormed furniture. As they crept in, a Japanese paper umbrella tumbled towards them. They gave themselves up to delighting in these treasures.

It was Johnny, to whom this place was not the stuff of dreams, who said rather obviously, "This must be in the theatre," and then disentangling Martin from a bearskin, added, "We'd better search for a way out. It'll be easier," he said, wrongly, "while the performance is still on." There was a phone call he wanted to make.

"I've just remembered," Martin said, putting down the bearskin in a demented sort of way.

"What?"

"That name outside. This is what my mum and dad were going to. They're out there."

There was no obvious way out. "Telephone," Johnny said, pointing.

"That's an idea!" Martin said. "I'll phone Ralph." Johnny wandered along the passage.

"Not in," Martin called to him. Johnny held up a hand for silence and pointed to a gold-painted door.

"My mum and dad are out there," Martin said. "That's why I could stay out this late. We've got to get out of here. We could get into really big trouble." There were butterflies in his stomach. He wished they had stayed in the flower shop, well away from this hazardous place. Johnny opened the gold door.

"We're walking into deadly danger," he whispered. He had got completely above himself. "Then we'll walk out the other side!"

"We can't risk it. No, *no!*" Martin hissed, trying to shock his friend back into his senses. Then they heard the footsteps, quick, sharp footsteps coming from the corridor that led to the Props Room. Without any hesitation they both bolted as fast as possible through the doorway.

They were in a vast, semicircular space, shadowy and edged round the arc with scaffolding. Dividing them from the other half of the circle, and the sea of the audience with Martin's parents in it, was a huge structure of boards painted to look like a brick wall, covered with peeling wallpaper and with aerosol messages so large and so uniformly clumsy that there was no possibility of forgetting it was a prop. A rosy pink light filtered over at the top of the towering wall. Martin glanced over towards the other side of the area, where an identical door led, apparently, into an identical passage. He saw a gold aerosol lying apparently discarded at his feet.

"Martin – *for Christ's sake!*" Johnny seemed momentarily to have recovered his senses. Martin was so excited now that all sense of his position had left him. He began to wave the aerosol in great arcs. Johnny grabbed at his arm. Martin pushed him away; and as Johnny came forward to grab at him again, turned the aerosol towards him menacingly. The rosy light went out, leaving them in complete darkness. The floor lurched under their feet, and a bar of dusky, almost velvety light appeared to their left. It began to broaden. From somewhere not very far away they heard a human voice hissing something at them.

"This way," Martin said quickly, and ran towards the scaffolding. As they reached the edge of the arc they had to jump. The floor was moving. Ten yards away, in the shadows, they saw the shape of a man. He saw them in the same instant.

"Hey!" he began. "What d'you think *you're* –"

Martin grabbed Johnny's wrist, and pulled him up the nearest ladder. The stage finished rotating: a room with peeling wallpaper, an ironing board, and a plastic baby in a cradle lay below them. As the curtain rose for the last act, the audience saw a new addition to the wall, drips already beginning to run from the letters:

GAY PRIDE '81

"How long've we been waiting now?"

"It's just past eleven," Martin said, looking at his watch.

"It's only an hour or so, then," Johnny said. "I thought it was more. Isn't it safe to move yet?"

"They might still be looking for us. They nearly got you, back there."

"What *are* we going to do, though?"

"We can't go anywhere near the stage. They're hunting us there if they're hunting us anywhere. We'll have to hunt around for a fire-escape or something."

"That'll make two fire-escapes in one day."

"I'll need a third if I don't get back home before my mum and dad do."

"I don't think you've got much chance. The play must've finished hours ago."

"They said they were getting the last train. If I can get that one maybe I can slip past them on the platform and run home before them and pretend I've been there ages."

"You should have done what I did and said you were staying the night over at a friend's."

"But I haven't *got* any friends, you idiot, except you, that I'd be *likely* to stay over with! And I couldn't say you because you'd already rigged your own excuse. Anyway, what *was* the point in rigging that one?"

"I was planning to stay out. Like Malcolm did."

"Jesus," Martin said.

"When is the last train, anyway?"

"I checked this morning. Half an hour. So we're going now." Martin swung himself out from the alcove down onto the highest plank of the scaffolding. Three ladders below he could see a window. Johnny joined him with a clatter. Some loose metal object, possibly a spanner, dislodged itself from the plank and spun off into the darkened abyss below. They stood paralysed for a full second: then a blinding white light glared up at them from the floor. A huge, angry roar from below commanded them to stop. Martin seemed to be going mad, he was rushing down the ladders *towards* the light.

"Keep your face turned away!" he hissed furiously at Johnny. The whisper, and the clatter of their descent, and the sound of more running feet below, reverberated in the huge space. A second torch beam shot up at them. Somebody was climbing the scaffolding towards them.

"Stay where you are!" roared the man on the floor. "Get up and bring them down, Mick."

The man called Mick had a third torch. He was only two floors of scaffolding below.

"The window won't open. It's stuck!" Martin gasped, terrified. He tugged at it, beginning to give way to panic. Things seemed to swim and turn black. He had an insane impulse to jump off the scaffolding and fly away. Johnny pulled at the window in a panic, feeling ready to scream.

"Right, you lads, stop right there," Mick said. "You're for it now."

The window flew open.

"Shut that," he ordered. "It's only a couple of kids," he called down. "I'll bring 'em down right away."

Martin swung himself out of the window. Johnny clambered onto the ledge after him.

There was no fire-escape.

"Come back here, or you're in real trouble!" Mick charged towards them, shouting. Then Martin saw the fire-escape – fifteen feet to the right, a forty foot drop below, and at the bottom a white face looking up at them. Their retreat was cut off.

Martin began to swing himself from side to side. Suddenly his hands stopped grasping the frame, and he threw himself to the right. Six feet down he struck the ledge he was aiming at. The window-box he landed on toppled over and crashed down towards the ground below, Martin with it. He could never remember how he managed to grasp the overflow pipe: it seemed automatic. His impetus tore his grip free, and sent him hurtling towards the fire-escape. The gold aerosol crashed against the ground below. He scrabbled at the rushing air, felt a hard bar against his fingertips for a split second: then he was flung against the railings, and onto the steps. All the breath had been driven from his body, but his fear got him to his feet and down the next thirty feet of the fire-escape. Five feet from the ground he started trembling so violently his legs folded under him. Someone grabbed him and held him tight. Then he blacked out. The last sound he heard was Mick weeping and raving at the window above.

Johnny stepped off the bottom of the drainpipe.

"Here! Get over here!" a voice hissed. He stumbled towards the voice, trod on the aerosol and automatically picked it up, staring stupidly at it. A hand grabbed his arm and pulled him into a taxi.

"Victoria, please, and fast as possible."

Johnny shook his head, felt for the door-handle. "Where's my friend –?" he began to mumble. "Wha –?"

"Martin's here," a voice said, shakily. "He's all right. No broken bones."

Johnny looked at the huddled figure of Martin, and saw who was holding him.

"*Ralph!*"

"That's right. I've been hanging round here for hours trying to find you. They let Annette out of the police-station. Maria's still in there. Annette said they hadn't got you. So I had to find out where you *were*. I've nearly got heart-failure."

"Is Martin all right?"

"He's ok. He's ok. No bones broken."

"No bones broken," Martin echoed, looking up a little.

"You're lucky you're alive." Ralph's face was screwed up with anxiety.

"No ... I was *trying* to get the fire-escape ... and I did ..." Martin had almost completely recovered. But it was still as if he were in a nightmare. "What's that clock say?" he demanded in sudden alarm. "What's the time?" His stomach jolted sickeningly.

"Quarter past twelve."

"How long have I been unconscious?"

"Less than a minute."

Martin felt caught in the nightmare. "But –" He looked at his watch. It indicated just past eleven. "Oh *God!*" he said. He had picked up the phrase from Ralph.

"Stop the taxi," Johnny said.

"What's wrong?"

"Stop the taxi. We can't get back."

They got out at Piccadilly Circus. There were bright lights and crowds everywhere, and appetising smells drifted through the air. "Hamburgers!" Johnny said. Martin looked hungrily at the nearest stall. Ralph marched them up to it and bought six hamburgers and two bottles of orangeade. The stall-keeper looked at him curiously. He was still wearing his clone uniform. They ate hungrily.

"Now what is all this?" Ralph said. Johnny explained about the last train back.

"Well, in that case there's only one thing to do," he said firmly. He led them to the nearest phone-booth.

"Hullo? Mrs Sutcliff? Hullo, this is Ralph speaking ... yes ... yes, he's here ... both of them ... we went to a film ... just missed the last train back. Couldn't get through to you before ... you've only just got in? That would account for it ... oh, the train *was* early leaving? I thought it must be ... oh, changed timetable? Well, really, the porters didn't seem to know anything about it ... typical British Rail ... yes, I'm bringing them home ... Which bus did you say? Splendid ... and change ... right. Yes, he's here ... over to you, Martin."

"Hullo Mum ... yes it was a good film ... yes, I'm coming straight back ... no, there's no point in staying up, is there? ... yes ... yes, I'll be quiet coming in ... yes, I've had a good time ... see you in the morning ... Bye."

"And that," said Ralph, "is that. Very neatly arranged. What film are you going to say you saw?"

Martin remembered a cinema they'd passed earlier that afternoon. "*Solo*," he said, "I've seen it before."

"An innocuous choice," Ralph approved. "We'd better get another taxi to the Embankment. We're catching the first of those buses there."

It had been a good day. Martin was feeling dazed and happy. His bruises were stiffening, and he was beginning to feel sleepy. He could see Johnny was sleepier: he was almost visibly nodding off, unless it was the motion of the bus ... Martin's own thoughts, and the excitement of a bus-ride late at night, kept him awake. He looked out through the black windows into deserted streets and at strange, tall buildings. Every so often they passed a tree, its leaves colourless in the lamplight, its branches dramatically lit curves, or a belated pedestrian – Martin wondered who it could possibly be. Brightly lit shops fleeted by, he'd never seen them before. He craned his head round curiously. Beside him, Ralph was sitting peacefully thinking about nothing. Johnny, too tired now even to yawn, drooped his head onto Ralph's shoulder, and fell asleep. But Martin was still happily daydreaming and staring out at the strange land they were passing through so fast for the next three-quarters of an hour.

"Terminus coming up now," Ralph said. "Excuse me," he said to the conductor. "But where do we catch the 199?"

"The 199?"

"Yes."

"Well, you don't. Not from here."

"But I thought we could change to it at the terminus?"

"Ah yes, but not *this* terminus. The route's been changed."

"Just a minute," Ralph said, staring out the window. "Just where are we now?"

"Well, you're about back in Lambeth, now."

"But we didn't want to go to Lambeth! We wanted to catch the 199!"

"Ah well then, you should've got off about ten stops back. Or eleven," he added meditatively. "You'd have to walk a good bit either way ..."

"I thought this bus went south."

"So it does, so it does, then north again to the terminus. And you did say it was the terminus you wanted. What? No, they changed the terminus over a year ago. I can't help that. I don't choose the route. No, you'll have to get off here. 'Night!"

"I should have thought of it," Ralph said bitterly. "What do they want to change these routes for anyway? I *thought* the places we were going through didn't seem familiar."

"What's happened?" Johnny asked sleepily.

"We're just as far away from home as when we started," Ralph said.

"Oh," Johnny said, sat down on a bench, and began to doze again. Martin looked about him, interested. This was an adventure. Ralph sat down on the bench heavily, took out Tonto to pet him, produced a hip-flask, drank from it, said "Oh God," and began, rather obviously, to think.

It was a warm, starry night. They were in an avenue of limes, lit by occasional silky-gold streetlights. Martin played with the white rat, drank orangeade, and felt in no hurry at all. He would like this to go on a long time. Johnny was happily asleep. Martin thought back over the events of the day: the beauty and excitement of the march; their arrival, as important couriers, at Hyde Park – the first to bring news of what had happened to their section of the march; the witty change Maria had thought of for that poster. It had been an offensive poster. He thought about that idea for a time, stopped to check Tonto from running off his knees, looked up at the velvety night and brilliant stars, and then his ideas became mixed up with reminiscences of that cascade of masks and bearskins and a genuine skull he wished he'd taken: he yawned, took a drink of orangeade and listened to crickets chirping on a nearby lawn.

"There's nothing for it," Ralph said, "but to go back into the city and find out where we can get a train most of the way – if we can. I'll get you a taxi at the other end. First we'd better find out exactly where we are. Wake up, Johnny!"

Johnny rubbed his eyes. "Where are we?" he asked. Martin thought this was funny.

"Here's someone coming," Ralph said. "You know, it's on occasions like this that it's inconvenient being a clone. I've had hundreds of suspicious glances already. I'm sure the police must've had dozens of accounts of suspected abduction –"

"– Why did you decide to be a clone, anyway?"

"The unrivalled roller-skating opportunities, chiefly ... oh."

A policeman strolled up to them. "Hullo," he said, "Hullo, hullo. Woss," he added genially, "all this then?" He chuckled at his own joke. "Been in some sort of competition, sir?"

"Sort of ... could you tell us where we are? We're trying to get back into the city."

"Ah. These two nippers are with you, then, sir, are they? And what are you two doing out so late?"

"We're trying to get back home."

"Ah, but that doesn't really answer my question, does it? What does that badge of yours say?" He put his hand on Johnny's badge and twisted it up to the light. "What's that, eh?" He looked at the lambda uncomprehendingly. "I see you've got the same, son. Is it a society?" He chuckled heartily, as if to conceal his careful examination of Martin's other badges. "Fesbian Leminists ... *Gay Pride '81*? What're you wearing a badge like that for? Was you on that march?" He chuckled again, and turned to Ralph. "Might I have your name, sir?" he said.

"Mike Abrams," Ralph said.

"Thank you sir, and the address?"

Ralph gave a false address.

"And your name, son?"

Martin and Johnny followed Ralph's example.

"Thank you," the policeman said, and lifted his radio to speak into it. "Three of them," they heard him say, though he had moved away a little, "names ... description, medium height, short fair hair ... roller skates, shorts ... dark hair, jeans ... check up please ... yes, I was thinking about that march ..."

"Now sir, would you mind telling me exactly what you're doing here?"

Ralph told him about the changed bus-route.

"That was a funny bus to take, if I may say so, sir."

"We didn't know about the change of route."

"So you say, sir."

"Can you tell us now where we are and how to get back into town? We're rather anxious to get a train before it's too late."

"Can you just tell me again what you were doing this afternoon, son?" the policeman asked Johnny.

"We went to a film."

"Which film was it?"

"*Solo*."

"Ah, and did you enjoy it? Have a good time?"

"Yes."

"I see. Where did you get those badges from? They're strange badges for lads your age to be wearing, you know."

"We've had them for ages," Martin said.

"Did you go to this film too?"

"Look," Ralph said, "Could you please tell us the best way to get back into the city? We need to get back in time for those trains."

"There's plenty of time, sir. No need to worry about that. There'll be a car along in a moment."

"A car?"

"Just to take you down to the station, sir. It'll be more comfortable there. Just routine, sir." The radio crackled. He moved away. They heard him say, "What's that? Could you repeat –?"

Johnny was suddenly convinced it was a message about them. He beckoned wildly at the other two, and set off at full pelt up the road.

"Hoi! Stop!" The policeman took a few steps after him, and then turned back towards Martin and Ralph. Martin ran, as fast as he could, in the opposite direction to the one Johnny had taken. Ralph followed him.

Martin realised that his fall had left him stiffer than he thought. The policeman, though he was quite old and Martin was a very good runner, was going to get him. It was a downhill run, and getting steeper. He looked round. The policeman was ten yards away. "Now then son," he called, "there's no call for that." Martin looked despairingly at the policeman, and made another dart downhill. He soon lost his lead. The policeman made a grab at him: and simultaneously Ralph swooped back on his roller-skates, gathered up Martin in a fireman's lift and whizzed downhill at a terrific rate.

"STOP!" the policeman bawled. "STOP!"

"GAY PRIDE!" Martin yelled back. "GAY PRIDE '81! SING IF YOU'RE GLAD TO BE GAY!" His voice diminished in the distance. The policeman did not sing.

They were gathering speed tremendously now. Martin saw the tree-tops flick past, and then the unchanging and brilliant stars. He felt Ralph sink into a crouch so as not to fall. It was a very steep hill. They swooped round a corner. Ralph only just avoided cannoning into a hedge. His swerve carried him dangerously near a parked car. Martin put his arms round Ralph's neck and clutched tight. They came to another sharp bend. The stars streamed overhead. Ralph gave his clone disco-whoop and narrowly escaped a lamp-post. Martin tried out a disco-whoop himself. He couldn't quite manage the gutturals at the beginning. The slope was beginning to flatten out. Dusky expanses of turf, a park of some sort, behind hooped railings, appeared on their right. In the distance they could see a line of silky gold lights indicating a road at the far border of the park. Ralph slackened his pace, twisted round to stop, and put Martin down.

"Come on," he said, "Over those railings as fast as you can – we'd better move. You heard what he said about that car." Martin scampered towards the shelter of the nearest bushes. Ralph took off his skates and ran barefoot, holding them in his hand, towards the line of lights.

"We've got to try and find Johnny," Martin said.

"That's why we're heading towards that road. It looks as if it's leading up to where we were. I *think* it's the one he ran down." He sounded very worried. "I hope to God he's all right. Oh God. I hope he hasn't gone back to where we were." He had to run fairly slowly so that Martin could keep up. "I'd never forgive myself."

"Where's Tonto?" Martin asked suddenly. Ralph's tired face turned to stare at him in the gloom.

"I thought you had him."

"No. I thought you did."

"Hell."

"We've got to find him. He'll starve, or a cat'll get him."

"Just at the moment," Ralph said, "I'm more concerned about finding Johnny."

They had arrived at the road, and Ralph was about to climb over the railings. Martin heard a low, urgent voice calling some distance away. He turned. The muffled voice spoke again. "*Hey!*" It seemed to come from the lower edge of the park. Ralph ran down the hill.

"Hey!"

"Johnny!" Ralph was ecstatic with relief. "Thank God for that."

"Is there any way round these bars?"

The park seemed to be divided in half by a much bigger fence of fifteen-foot bars. Beyond them was Johnny, a group of mysterious buildings, and then more parkland.

"What are you doing in there?"

"I climbed up by that tree and dropped in. But I can't get out that way."

"But why did you go in?"

"To get away from that policeman. Where is he?"

"He chased us. We left him standing. But more might have turned up by now."

"There's plenty of places to hide in here. It's all right, Tonto. It's all right."

"Tonto! Have you got Tonto there?"

"Yes. I picked him up when I scarpered."

Tonto was passed through the bars and petted. He seemed to be enjoying himself.

"I've got your orangeade," Martin said.

"Great!" The two boys drank orangeade and played with Tonto.

"Orangeade," the Lone Clone said. "Orangeade. How you two manage this sort of thing on orangeade beats me." He produced his hipflask and took a long draught of something that restored him to his normal cheeerfulness. "You must have nerves of steel," he said happily.

"Tonto likes crawling up people's sleeves," Johnny told him inconsequentially.

"Well, if you can't get out of there," Ralph said, "we'd better climb in. It's best if we're all together, and I rather like the idea of bars like that between me and the police."

"Why did you give a false name?" Martin asked.

"We've been in trouble, and Jesus knows what you've got up to, this afternoon. If they checked up afterwards they couldn't pester us. It was just our bad luck he decided to check up now."

"But what did he want to take us down the station for?"

"That's obvious," Johnny said.

"He wouldn't have done that if it'd been two girls with you," Martin said.

"He most certainly would."

"That's not very likely," Johnny said.

"It is, I tell you. Look, it was the badges did for us. No policeman believes gays can ever be friends. If I want to know their opinions, I read the letters in *Men Only*."

"That's why we've got to have demos," Martin said.

Though it was a quarter past three by Martin's corrected watch, it was still almost as warm as a Mediterranean summer night. The scents of turf and flowering trees were wafted across the park. Somewhere near the glow of the city on the sky-line of the park, birds were singing. From south of there they heard a confused murmur like traffic or an evening street. Something was happening. They stopped to sit down again, and let Tonto run on the grass. They decided that this part of the park must be private, and the buildings in it perhaps offices of some sort: but there seemed to be no sign of a caretaker, or dogs. Probably, Ralph said, if there was a caretaker he was there simply to ring the police or fire-brigade in an emergency, and not to patrol the grounds himself. But perhaps they had better, once they were all rested, move into the public part of the park, and lurk till they could find out where they were. They were lying on their backs staring up at the sky thick with stars. Martin was asleep now, and so was Johnny. Ralph shook them after a while.

"I wasn't asleep," Martin said. "We'd better move on."

"That's what I was thinking."

Johnny yawned and rubbed his eyes. "Hullo Tonto," he said, "Don't shake me like that ... oh it's you mum – Martin – oh, are we going on?" He woke up fully.

"We can get over by those trees," Ralph said.

It was from the top of the railings that Martin saw what lay ahead.

"Look! A lake! A lake!" The water was smooth as glass and stretched for a hundred yards – big enough to be called a lake, in London.

"Swings," Ralph said, spotting a set of graceful angular structures on a rise nearby. Martin and Johnny jumped down eagerly and ran to the shore. Ralph walked more sedately, being barefoot, to the swings, and leaning back pushed himself to and fro until he saw the stars stream above him. As he swung higher, he saw at each moment of motionlessness upside-down leaves suspended, very clear-cut and still as if in water, imprinted on the bowl of bright stars. He heard the clacking of the roundabout whirling round with Johnny on it. Next Ralph tried the slide several times. He felt very peaceful, and with it was beginning to feel tired. It was nearly four o'clock. Surely that was *music* he had just heard wafted on the wind? They had best, he thought, wait now until about five or six, and then find the nearest station and take the first train south. Or was it just London sounds of night, confused on the breeze?

Martin came up from the shore with Tonto on his shoulder. "There're *boats* down there!" he said.

"Are there?" Ralph asked peacefully.

"I'm going out on the lake."

"Hey," Ralph protested. "Not in someone else's boat. We've had enough trouble for one night."

"There's a canoe"

"*No.*"

"– and it's untied. Now," he added. "It's big enough for three. Come on!"

Even when he was wide awake, Ralph wasn't capable of arguing for long: he was too easily talked over: besides, the strangeness of the idea attracted him. Johnny leapt from the swing. They walked down to the shore, and embarked on the dark, starry water. The wind had vanished: it was a profoundly still night. The silence was interrupted only by the quiet splash of the paddles, and the occasional faint, unidentifiable sounds that drifted over whenever there was a slight disturbance of the air. They, three of them in the canoe, the bubbles splashing at the paddles, and the ripple of their wake, were the only moving thing on the glassy water bordered by bullrushes and dark turf, from which rose shadows up to the brilliant sky. The lake was much longer than it had seemed. They passed the buildings, tall rectangles cut out of the span of stars, and the feathery silhouettes of trees; and then they saw, blocking out the sky beyond the high railings, an immense floating shape: they might have thought they were dreaming if it were not for the dim lights, the first they had seen since they entered the park, shining up from the turf below. It was the sleepiness beginning to master Ralph and the dreamlike quality so much more accessible to the young in Martin and Johnny, that let them so easily accept, almost without surprise, that a huge balloon was towering above them in the night sky.

Martin turned the boat towards the shore, and grounded it in the bullrushes.

"What's that?" Ralph asked, waking up a little.

"I want to have a closer look at that," Martin told him. He stepped from the boat and ran up the slope to a tree by the railings. The others followed him more slowly.

"Haven't you caused enough confusion for one night?" Ralph said, clutching a branch while he upended his hipflask again. "WHAT!" Martin's plan had nearly made him fall out of the tree. "No, no, *no!* Besides," he added, cheering up, "There's no paint to do it with."

Martin laughed: and flourished his gold aerosol.

"Stand by! Ready to catch?"

"Got it!"

"Aim that floodlight back, Johnny ... Right," called Ralph, "We'd better loose all the ropes at once, if we're going to do it."

"We've got to," Martin said, dropping back to earth, "Otherwise when they get round to launching it they'll just see the difference and not let it off till they've changed it back."

"Yes, I see that," Ralph said. "But when it goes, we run for it, right?"

"Yes, of course. There'll be people along to investigate in no time."

"Right. Just a moment – you ready? Right –" he fumbled at the knots. "Done it ... Ok round your side?"

"Just a minute," Johnny called. "Buzz over your knife, Martin –"

"For Christ's sake! *Hurry!*"

"Ok – right! Cast off!"

They leapt back and the balloon shot thirty feet into the air.

"Run away! *Run away!*" Ralph scrambled up the branches onto the railings, laughing madly. "Scarper!" Martin gasped, scrabbling up after him. "Messer Rondo forever!"

"The Lone Clone fights on!" Ralph cried, falling off the railings and rolling down towards the lake.

"Look," Johnny called, "Tarzan!" He grabbed hold of a dangling rope and swung himself off the railings. The rope moved on.

"Let go you silly bugger," Ralph called. "Let go!"

The balloon moved on majestically, forty feet up in the air, Johnny dangling fifteen feet below.

"Who d'you think you are, bleeding Montgolfier?" Ralph shouted.

"Let go when you get over the lake!" Martin called. "We'll row out and rescue you!"

Johnny shouted horrible curses back. The balloon was gathering height very slowly if at all: but it was moving faster across the park. Ralph set off to run round the lake after it: Martin fell into the canoe, and paddled furiously on the track of the balloon. Johnny was waving wildly to them and imitating Ralph's disco-whoops. He had got above himself, Martin thought. He decided to tell this joke to Ralph.

"Come down out of that!" Ralph was calling. "Look, everybody's going to try and catch that balloon. You don't want to be found on it!" He turned back to the lake. "Come *on*, Martin!" Johnny was swinging about on the end of the rope, either in an attempt to guide the balloon or out of sheer high spirits.

"Good thing it was hardly inflated," Ralph said. "It'll come down in the next half-mile. Where's it going to take us before that, that's what I'd like to know."

"I still think –" Martin began, and doubled up laughing.

"Stop it, stop it! We've made enough noise to wake every policeman in Basingstoke."

"Basingstoke?"

"We don't want them *as well*." Ralph fell flat on his face.

"It's a pity really," Martin said, "it *wasn't* full of hydrogen.

They'd never have got it down and everyone would've seen it."

"Just as well for Johnny – Look, it's heading for those trees! Run! keep an eye out just in case anybody does turn up."

They ran. A violent struggle seemed to be taking place in the upper branches. Odd twigs and leaves were being hurled out.

"Look," Martin said. "There's a really funny monkey in that tree."

"Very funny," Johnny said sourly.

"That's what I said."

"Stand aside! I'm coming down." He fell out of the tree. "That was brilliant! It's the best ride I ever had! When I'm grown up," he added, "I'm going to buy a balloon –"

The balloon, released from Johnny's weight, rose up above the tree: the rope slithered away from the branches.

"Now I know what a kite feels like," Johnny said ecstatically.

"Look!" Ralph said. The balloon had risen fifty feet into the air. They looked up reverentially at the words on the front and back: MOTHER'S PRIDE in big black letters, and through the first word, a neat streak of gold, and above, in big letters, a golden GAY.

GAY
PRIDE
'81

"It's nearly five o'clock," Ralph said. "Let's get out of here and onto the streets. It should be safe enough now."

They started walking shakily towards the distant railings, perfectly visible now under an increasingly lightening deep-blue sky. The morning stars shone faintly.

The music festival had stopped hours ago, but even now one or two low-voiced groups sat together mildly strumming at their guitars, enjoying a last drink or smoke, engaged in desultory conversation about dawn, food, spirits, music and personal affairs. A band was discussing, for the hundredth time, their new lyric. Someone was talking about Sibelius. They hardly looked up at the barefoot man carrying roller-skates, or the two children.

"Where's the station, do you know? The railway station?"

"It's down the end of that road, right? Just walk along. It's about two minutes away."

"Great! Do you know when the next train south is?"

"About half an hour ... I'm going on it myself. We're just packing up, you see." He looked at Ralph with dawning interest.

"Wait a bit! Weren't the pigs after you a bit earlier?"

"Well –"

"Yes, they came round here looking for you all. It was a bad scene. What the hell's *that*?" His voice rose. The balloon, driven by a changing gust of wind, was swooping down on them.

"Er –"

"You'd better shift off to the station. There's still pigs around, keeping an eye on us. Look out!"

He yelled the last words. The first policemen appeared hopping over the railings on the far side of the park. Everybody jumped to their feet.

"*Run away!*" Ralph yelled. "*Run away!*" Martin and Johnny were already scrambling over the railings. The festival scattered in all directions, all except the band. They weren't going to leave their speakers.

"Right," an impassioned voice cried. "This is where we get to play that song –" The huge drum resounded, and the group burst into a demonic performance of "Here Come the Pigs". It was the right occasion.

"Quick, over the big railings," a rainbow-haired girl called to her boyfriend.

"I've found a boat!" another voice called.

"It's this way," said Eric, the man who'd given the alarm, to Ralph. The Lone Clone was whizzing along on his restored roller-skates.

"We're in here!" Martin called. The last sounds of "Here Come the Pigs" died away. Three men with a guitar, a violin and a flute ran past. "They've got a coffee machine."

"Yes, three please," Ralph was saying at the counter. "Better carry your coffee down to the platform!" he called. The morning was quite cold: the sky was completely light now, but there was no sunshine yet.

"Good festival, was it?" the porter said.

"Yes, thank you," Martin replied politely.

"I never got to anything like that when I was your age."

Johnny was staring up at the pale blue sky and the small white fleecy clouds chasing westwards. He thought he could see them gleaming in the sun. Suddenly – "Look!" he called. "Look!" – pointing upwards.

"Well there you are then," the porter said. The balloon was towering sixty feet above them. "GAY," it said, "~~MOTHER'S~~ PRIDE '81."

"You can keep Tonto," the Lone Clone said, "if you want.

I'm getting a kitten."

"*Can* I? That would be great!"

"Mind your coffee. Well," Ralph sighed, "I'm all for a quiet life after this."

"My mum and dad'll be really surprised when they see him." Johnny looked up for a moment almost wistfully at the sunlit clouds. The rat, sitting on his neck, preened itself.

The train drew in. "Oh, come on!" Martin protested as he stepped on, steadying his coffee. "You're going to have to put off your quiet life. You can't expect one really, not with six whole weeks of the holidays to go. See you tomorrow!"

The train started up.

"See you tomorrow!"

The Authors

STEPHEN AIREY lives in Cambridge. As well as writing he paints pictures and is a member of the arts workshop group CADRE. His chief occupation is sitting in pubs. Cider (should readers wish to buy him a pint) is what he drinks.

TOM CLARKSON is a writer and painter. His previous publications include: *The Pavement and the Sky, Love is My Vocation, The Wounded* (soon to be republished), *A Certain Summer, The Dirty Workers, Tarot – The Life-Enhancer*, and a book of poems *Angel of My Bed*.

JOHN GOWLING was born in Inner City Manchester in 1952, where he still lives in a condemned high-rise flat; and has worked in a night club, mail room, hospital and on the buses. He has had gay writing published in *Voices* and by the Manchester-based writing group Commonword, who are publishing his gay novel *Marshall's Big Score*. In 1981, with the help of author Ian Everton he set up Northern Gay Writers who have recently published their first anthology.

MICHAEL JAMES is a war-time love-child whose natural talents were subverted and almost destroyed by the indoctrination into catholicism at two primary schools not worth mentioning and one grammar school going under the name of Saint Boniface. At the age of 42 he is tentatively trying to rediscover his lost talents, if any, before it is too late.

TENEBRIS LIGHT was born in Iraq in 1946. He is the co-founder of Brilliance Books gay press and lives in London with his lover Roy Trevelion. His previous publications include *Three Rainbows*, of which he is very proud, and *Kleek Poems*, a collection of juvenilia whose mere mention causes him extreme embarrassment.

PAUL MANN did two years National Service in the Royal Marines by mistake, and has had several sundry jobs, including eleven years at sea as a deputy purser. He has an interest in Yoga and lives mostly a quiet life in Sussex.

CHRIS PAYNE is a Northerner settled in London. He's in his late twenties and this is his first published work. He enjoys reading detective stories and playing football.

DAVID REES lives in Devon and teaches at Exeter University. His novels include the bestselling *The Milkman's On His Way, In The Tent*, and *The Estuary*. In 1977 he won the Carnegie Medal for *The Exeter Blitz*, and in 1980 the Other Award for *The Green Bough of Liberty*.

PETER ROBINS' work has appeared in magazines in Britain, Holland, Sweden, the United States and Australia. Other publications include *Doves for the Seventies* (poems; 1970), *Undo Your Raincoats and Laugh* (gay short stories; 1977), *The Gay Touch* and *Our Hero Has Bad Breath* (gay short stories; both 1982); and he is a contributor to the anthologies *Cracks in the Image* and *On the Line* (both 1981). He is a working journalist and lives in South London.

Gay Men's Press is an independent publishing project set up to produce books relevant to the male gay movement and to promote the ideas of gay liberation.

OTHER FICTION TITLES

Richard Dipple (ed.)
Cracks in the Image

16 short stories by 13 British and American writers, including Barry Nonweiler, Peter Robins, Ian Everton, Jon Ward and David Rees. 'The Gay Life as she is lived. There will be few readers who don't find themselves in at least one of these miniatures' (*Gay News*).

Barry Nonweiler
That Other Realm of Freedom

Glasgow, London and New Zealand form the backdrop to Simon's quest for freedom in a novel that fearlessly holds a mirror to gay oppression. 'The reader will be dazzled by his intricacy and the extent of thematic concern' (*Gay Community News*, Melbourne).

Giovanni Vitacolonna
A Sweet and Sour Romance

How do you keep a relationship going, or just your emotional balance, on the fast-moving gay scene of today? These are among Sal's problems as he plunges into the sexual whirlpool of San Francisco, then off in search of a new life in Italy. Sparkling, insightful and hilarious.

Ian Everton
Alienation

A highly emotive novel from the gay movement, set in a gay group struggling for survival in a homophobic North of England city. Like their new-found friends, lovers Peter and Jon seek to make a better life for themselves, but the real and ideal worlds rarely coincide.

David Rees
The Estuary

Cheryl felt she could do worse than marry fading pop star Aaron after Luke and she split up; and hadn't Luke suprised everyone by finding a new lover in John? Increasingly caught up in their network are Jack and Kevin, at a stalemate in their own relationship and looking for ways to branch out . . .

The Estuary – a novel of contemporary lives, where sex and friendship can find many combinations.

Our full catalogue is available from:
Gay Men's Press
P O Box 247
London N15 6RW
England.
For mail order add 10% of list price.